THE QUEEN'S EYE

To Peggy—
My fellow Gardener.
Thanks!
Jane

THE QUEEN'S EYE

Jane Alden

Desert Palm Press

The Queen's Eye
(A Cass & Ari Adventure – Book 2)

By Jane Alden

©2024 Jane Alden

ISBN (book): 9781954213845
ISBN (epub): 9781954213852

For permission requests, write to the publisher at lee@desertpalmpress.com or "Attention: Permissions Coordinator," at

Desert Palm Press
1961 Main Street, Suite 220
Watsonville, California 95076
www.desertpalmpress.com

Editor: Heather Flournoy
Cover Design: TreeHouse Studio

Printed in the United States of America
First Edition June 2024

Acknowledgment

A thousand thanks to beta readers. They encourage us when we stall, keep us on track when we stray, and provide the most important perspective of all...will a reader really enjoy our tales. Special thanks from Nefertiti to Donna Connally, Kim Dyke, and Patricia Adams Clark.

Prologue

The Royal City Of Akhetaten, Egypt

1336 BCE

OMARI HUMMED A HALF-remembered nursery song in his head in rhythm with the back-and-forth of the palm fan. His job was keeping flies from bothering Master Thutmose while the sculptor worked on the bust of the queen. A dry desert breeze blew in the east-facing window of the workshop carrying the sick-sweet smell of animal hides boiling in the black iron glue kettle outside. Omari swallowed hard. The odor roiled his stomach.

Sometimes the Master allowed Omari to do more important tasks than shooing flies like fetching the little crocks of color pigment and glue pots from the high shelves in the corner of the workroom. Omari would pull his stool across the hard-packed dirt floor being careful to raise as little dust as possible, climb up to the shelf, and reverently lift the vessel and carry the paint to the sculptor's workbench. From his earliest memory he could guess which color the artist would call for. The Master would ask for red for a man's flesh, blue for the river and the sky, yellow for the sun god Aten, black for evil and darkness.

Omari felt proud of his Master, one of the most important men in the new imperial city of Akhetaten. King Akhenaten personally bestowed an honorific title on the sculptor, King Akhenaten's Favorite, The Sculptor Thutmose. The honor would follow his Master through life. The King would allow Thutmose to commission artists to paint the title on the walls of his own tomb in the necropolis on the west bank of the Nile, across from the royal city.

On this day, the Master was working on a very important project. Omari remembered when Thutmose began the design for

Nefertiti's bust. First the artist drew a grid on papyrus paper. The height and width of each square was the length of his thumb as was the custom. He would use the grid as a guide for exactly the right proportions as he began chiseling the Queen's likeness from white limestone mined from cliffs above the river.

All day Thutmose had labored over a drawing of the life-sized shoulders and head of a woman. That night as the sun dipped into the Nile, the sculptor was still bent over the papyrus. He lit an olive oil lamp and leaned closer to the paper. "Go to bed, Omari. The flies are sleeping. Come early in the morning."

Before sunup the next day, Omari found the sculptor asleep with his head resting on the drawing. It was the face of the most beautiful woman Omari had ever seen, a vision of a regal lady with high cheekbones, a long, graceful neck, and almond-shaped eyes.

Day after day Omari watched the artist transform the flat representation on the papyrus into the beautiful three-dimensional image of Queen Nefertiti in her blue crown and brightly colored collar.

"Master, the fresh glue is ready." A voice in the open doorway made Omari jump and brought him back from musing about the past. A gangly youth hesitated on the threshold. He held out a glue pot. "Will you test it?" Seamon was twelve years old to Omari's ten years and stood a head taller. The older boy considered Omari his rival for Thutmose's attention. At night when the workers tucked themselves into their bedrolls, Seamon used the meaning of Omari's name, He Who Is Highborn, to tease him. He called the younger boy Little Prince. Omari had no memory of his life before the sculptor's workshop beyond snatches of nursery rhymes, and he sometimes had vague dreams of a beautiful dark-skinned woman singing to him in the night. Maybe that was his mother.

The Master beckoned Seamon. "Come in, boy. Bring me the pot."

Seamon crossed the room, placed the gluepot on the workbench, and backed away three steps. Thutmose took the pot, smelled it, and swirled the gelatinous fluid. "The glue looks perfect, Seamon. Well done."

Seamon smirked at Omari. "Thank you, Master." He backed out the door carrying the smell of the fire and boiling skins with him.

Thutmose consulted the papyrus grid to his left on the workbench. He gently caressed the bust, running the back of his hand across her high cheekbone and lips, slightly upturned in a serene smile. He whispered, "You're almost finished, my gorgeous Queen."

Omari looked around the shop at the other stone images of famous people and members of the royal court. "She is your most beautiful work. Will she be in a tomb or a temple?"

"She is not for a temple or tomb, Omari. The King has commissioned her for his royal apartments. It's a great honor He has bestowed upon us. She must be perfect."

A chill ran down Omari's back. The Master had said "us." Did he mean Omari was part of the great honor too?

"Only the most important step remains. I must place her eyes through which she will gaze into eternity." He stirred the glue pot with a small brush and pointed across the room with the tip. "Bring me the little chest."

Omari lifted the small rosewood chest with Thutmose's name inscribed on the top and carried it to the workbench. He peered over the sculptor's shoulder as he opened the lid. Two perfect rock crystal eyes with black pupils stared back. Thutmose painted the Queen's empty right socket with glue. He carefully lifted the eye from the chest and pressed it in place.

Her face seemed to come to life. Omari held his breath and waited for her to speak. A shout from outside broke the spell. Thutmose and Omari rushed to the doorway and saw a dozen soldiers with drawn swords shove Seamon to the ground and upend the glue cauldron, dumping the boiling liquid on the sand.

Thutmose pushed Omari away from the door. "Get under the workbench."

"Who are they, Master?"

"Do as I say. Hurry."

Omari scrambled under the table and tried to make himself as small as possible. The soldiers crowded into the workroom. Omari could see their feet in worn, dusty sandals. They must have marched a long distance.

Thutmose's voice. "How dare you? Do you know who I am? I am the Favorite of the King." The sculptor's words were defiant but his voice shook. His tone made Omari shrink closer against the mud brick wall.

"I know who you are, Thutmose. The heretic King is dead and His harlot Great Wife with him. Praise be to all the Gods."

Thutmose let out a groan. "Does that mean I am to die too?"

"Don't flatter yourself. Get your tools together. The High Priest of Amun has summoned you north to Memphis."

"What of all my workers? Will they go with me to Memphis?"

"The new King has ordered them in the opposite direction, south to Thebes where He will restore the old ways and rebuild the temples Akhenaten and Nefertiti abandoned. Your workers are needed for making a new Theban necropolis on the west bank dedicated to the true Gods. The priests have already named the hallowed ground the Valley of the Kings."

The captain shoved Thutmose toward the door and spoke to the other soldiers. "We've wasted enough time with him. You two take him to the boat. The rest of you destroy everything."

The soldiers began sweeping all the sculptures of the King and noblemen and women from the shelves onto the dirt floor and smashing them to pieces with the hilts of their swords. From under the table Omari watched Thutmose's beautiful, perfect bust of Nefertiti fall face-first into the dust. A soldier knelt to finish her destruction and spied Omari cowering under the table. "Well, look what we have here." He grabbed Omari's leg to drag him out. The rough hand felt like a vise around Omari's thigh. Omari kicked as hard as he could with his free leg. The blow landed in the soldier's crotch. He let out a howl and tried to scramble under the workbench after the boy.

The captain kicked a broken piece of sculpture at the soldier. "Never mind him. Get on your feet. We're leaving."

As quickly as they came, they were gone. Omari climbed from under the table and looked around the workroom at the wreckage and Nefertiti's beautiful statue on the dirt floor. Seamon came to the door. His face was bloody from a deep cut on his forehead. Omari found a cloth the sculptor used to clean his brushes. "Here. You need to stop the bleeding."

Seamon held the cloth to his forehead and slumped to the floor. "What do we do now?"

Omari knelt and gently righted Nefertiti's bust. She was unharmed except for a few chips off her ears and a crack in the edge of her tall crown. He picked up the little rosewood chest from the dust and opened it. Nefertiti's crystal left eye gazed up at him. He ran his thumb across Thutmose's name on the chest's lid. "The captain said we're supposed to go to Thebes. The Queen is too heavy for me to carry, but I can save the papyrus and the eye." He rolled the papyrus as tightly as he could and stuck it and the chest inside his linen shirt. "If we leave now before the soldiers come back, we can make our own way to Thebes."

* * * * *

The sun's first rays shining through the roof opening over the kitchen area made a yellow square on the dirt floor. The other workers' soft rustling noises signaled it was time for Omari to prepare for the day. He touched the small wooden chest and papyrus under his pillow and ran his finger across Thutmose's name incised on the chest's lid. He did this every morning like a ritual to reassure himself they were still there. Beside him, Seamon murmured something unintelligible in his sleep. Omari nudged him. "Wake up. We have to go to work."

Seamon opened his eyes and rubbed the scar on his forehead. "Good morning, Little Prince." Over their two years in Thebes, the tone of Seamon's nickname for Omari had changed from a cruel taunt to an affectionate tease. They rolled their beds and grabbed their breakfast, a flat bread pancake and a cup of warm sweet beer. Seamon elbowed Omari in the ribs. "Remember when we were with Thutmose? We had honey with our bread."

"Of course I remember."

The boys followed the rest of the workers outside to the main road bisecting Pa Dem village. Seventy mud brick houses huddled tightly packed behind a high enclosure wall. The town was home to artists, craftsmen, and laborers building the elaborate Valley of the Kings tombs across the Nile from Thebes.

Since coming to Thebes, Omari had served as Menes's apprentice. Menes was the principal artist painting the walls of Tutankhamen's tomb where the new King would spend eternity. Menes was not a patient teacher. He expected Omari to keep the clay lamp filled with olive oil and burning brightly in the pitch-black tomb underground and to provide bowls of fresh water for Menes to drink and to clean his brushes. Whatever Omari learned of the techniques for making the beautiful pictures covering the tomb's walls was up to the boy, with no help from the artist.

Omari watched Menes create the colorful figures illustrating the King's life and his journey through the afterlife. With any stolen free moments he practiced the brush strokes on flat rocks with pigment from one of the painter's discarded pots. The most difficult part was divining the meanings of symbols that stood for spoken words. After two years in the tomb, he could read most of the stories.

"Hey, Menes. Did you hear the latest?" Konos was a journeyman craftsman who worked beside the artist, coloring inside the outlines of Menes's works. He idolized the artist and wanted to impress him, and gossip was his favorite pastime. Menes didn't respond. Konos pushed on. "Yes. The King is moving his father's coffin from his tomb near the abandoned northern capital to the Valley here. He'll be put in that old empty tomb down the way. The unfinished one. They say Akhenaten's already on a barge coming up the river. He'll be here in a few days."

Menes rested his brush on a bowl's lip and wiped his hands. "Yes, I know. And it's no business of yours. Pay attention to your work."

Another artist down the line spoke. "They say the tomb walls won't be painted with Akhenaten's story. The King decreed this disrespect because the old King angered god Amun. Akhenaten declared illegal the worship of any god but Aten."

Konos sneered. "More likely because the dead King angered Amun's priests. They stopped reaping the riches they were used to. I heard some of the priests live almost as lavishly as the King himself."

Menes threw down the rag. "Enough. You are worse than chattering old women squatting by the well wasting time gossiping. The vizier will be here soon checking our work, and I won't be criticized because of your idle babble."

That night Omari couldn't sleep. Light from a full moon streamed through the roof. An occasional cough punctuated the soft snores of workers scattered around the room. He ran his hand under his pillow and along the chest's edge. A picture of Thutmose's special gift for King Akhenaten, the beautiful bust of Nefertiti, flashed across his memory. If Thutmose were still alive he must be very sad thinking of the old King's fate. Omari made a decision. The papyrus and the Queen's eye belonged with Akhenaten in his new resting place.

Omari crawled from his bed and tucked the papyrus and chest into his loincloth's waistband. He tiptoed around the sleeping bodies and out the door into the street. He turned north toward the gap in the village wall. At the opening he paused in the shadows and listened for sounds of anyone stirring. A sand fox's shriek in the desert broke the stillness. The scream sounded like a child crying out in pain.

Outside the wall he ran across the open desert to a path around the mountain's flank that led to the tombs. Even without the full moon's light his feet would have known the way. At Tutankhamun's tomb entrance he paused at the top of the steps and peered into the blackness. He pictured the worksite inside the tomb where he had left the lamp with Menes's paints at day's end. He carefully descended the steps, hugging the rock wall. After a few stumbles he found the clay lamp and a flint lighter, a paint pot, and a brush, and made his way back toward the moonlight at the entrance.

Farther along the path a rubble pile marked the opening to the humble tomb King Tutankhamun meant for his father if the gossip were true. Omari climbed over the rocks. He stopped to light the lamp and descended twenty-one steps into the dank interior. A long passageway through an antechamber led to a small burial chamber. A damp puff of wind sent a shiver down the boy's back and caused the lamp's flame to dance. He held the lamp over his head, searching for a hiding place for the papyrus and chest. One of the paving stones near the corner of the burial chamber wall looked movable.

The gray glow at the tomb's entrance was already beginning to lighten with the approaching dawn. He'd have to hurry. He burned precious minutes struggling with the heavy stone. He found a piece of wood to use as a lever. He inched the paver aside and hollowed out a space in the sand beneath to hide first the papyrus then the chest on top of it. He strained to slide the stone back in place and knelt at the wall to begin painting the story of Thutmose's final gift to the old King, his Queen's eye.

Chapter One

Columbia University, New York City

1972

THE MAIN READING ROOM of Butler Library was practically deserted. Just me, a lone librarian, and eight or ten other souls scattered around heavy oak tables lining the massive hall. Classes would start in a week, and there wouldn't be an empty chair in the place. The librarian was trying to keep busy. She straightened already precisely aligned chairs around my table and gave me a quick little uncertain smile. Maybe she was new to Columbia too. I was familiar with the campus, of course. I had spent four undergraduate years across Broadway at Barnard. Or as my gran in North Carolina would say, "Just over yonder." Familiar old Barnard might be right across the avenue, but I felt unsettled. My world was turned upside down over the summer, and starting a Master's program in creative writing at Columbia this fall would certainly begin another new chapter. That's what I was doing in Butler Library the week before classes started, moving on from the events of the summer and getting a jump on my life's next chapter.

I opened my bookbag and slid *Finer Elements of Creative Writing* onto the table. "Chapter One. A Robust Outline: Your Story Arc's Best Friend." This wasn't starting out well. First of all, I hate the word robust. It's overused by people trying to sound smart. Second, how does a story arc have a friend?

I stared at the first paragraph for about ten minutes trying to focus. Life-sized portraits of King George II and his wife Queen Caroline gazed critically down at me from the reading room's south wall. You may wonder what a gigantic portrait of an English king is doing in the Butler Library reading room. I did. I looked it up. George chartered Columbia as King's College in 1754, twenty years before his crazy grandson, George III, caused the American Revolution. Grandpa wasn't so normal himself. He ordered the sides of his and Caroline's coffins removed so their remains "could mingle." I shifted in my chair and went back to trying to concentrate on Robust Outlines.

"Ari. Is that you Ari?" It was Eleanor Frame, a Barnard professor. "I thought it was you, but you look different." She pulled me out of my chair and hugged me hard. I smelled the expensive perfume she always wears, and memories of our six-month affair last year came crowding back. My nose is like that. Smells evoke pictures so vivid that it's almost like looking at a scrapbook of the past. Eleanor is the world's expert on Virginia Woolf and a terrific teacher. Her class, Modernist Women Authors of the Early Twentieth Century, is always full of adoring young women. The gossip is she picks out a senior each semester for a special relationship. I was the lucky dog the last semester before graduation.

She held me at arm's length. "I see being with Cass Stillwell agrees with you. You look great."

Eleanor introduced Cass and me while she was breaking up with me at the end of the semester, I suspect because she wanted me off her conscience. She recommended I apply to be Cass's assistant for a summer expedition to Luxor, Egypt.

Before I go on, I should probably pause and back up a bit. Dr. Cassandra Stillwell is a noted Egyptologist. She holds a doctorate from Oxford and an adjunct professorship at Columbia University. She's famous for finding the mummy of Hatshepsut, ancient Egypt's only real legitimate female pharaoh, lost for three thousand years. If you think I sound proud of Cass, I plead guilty. Before Cass, the Egyptology establishment, mostly old white men, questioned whether Hatshepsut even existed and pooh-poohed the idea that she reigned over the most successful period in Egypt's history.

The most credit they would give Hatshepsut was for being the regent to her infant stepson who inherited the throne at two years old. But Cass didn't believe Hatshepsut settled for being Number Two. Thanks to Cass's research and relentless sleuthing, we found her mummy. Our expedition proved she took on the traditionally male role of pharaoh by affecting physically masculine traits and male garb. Today, Hatshepsut lies serenely in the Egyptian Museum's main exhibit hall in Cairo, a proven real pharaoh. So you can see why I'm proud of Cass.

I helped her find Hatshepsut and, well, we have what you'd call a personal relationship too. I fell for her the first time I saw her in the Museum of Modern Art in New York before we went to Egypt to find the female pharaoh. Cass was standing in front of Hatshepsut's statue with her eyes closed, humming. I thought that was weird at the time, but her strange behavior didn't keep me from being hooked. I can still recall the feeling that day, my heartbeat speeding up and my mouth suddenly going dry.

Cass is beautiful. She's tall and thin with dark shoulder-length hair and dark eyes you could drown in. She's the kind of beautiful that makes you want to stand up straight and tuck your shirt in.

We got close during the trip to Luxor in search of Hatshepsut, but it took a while. If you met me, you'd assume I'd be bold about approaching someone. Let's just say I have an assertive look on the exterior. But the truth is I tend to hang back till I'm sure. With Cass I hesitated even though she was giving me all kinds of signals—touching and kissing. Cass made the first move. She's pretty much the top in our relationship. Fine with me.

Eleanor picked up my textbook and bookbag. "Let's go outside so we can talk. That librarian is giving us a look. I'll buy you a coffee."

We passed sunbathers scattered around the lawn in front of the library trying to hold on to their summer tans as long as possible. I followed Eleanor to a coffee kiosk with some café tables and chairs with spindly metal legs.

"This is better." She looked around. "More private." She pulled out a chair for me. "You sit here with your back to the sun. I have sunglasses." She fished tortoiseshell Guccis out of her bag. "So, I've seen Cass all over TV. She looks wonderful. She's famous, of course, for her discovery. Is she coming back to Columbia?"

"For now, she's committed to staying in Cairo to help the Ministry of Antiquities examine every inch of the golden coffin and Hatshepsut's mummy. After that, it's kind of up in the air."

Eleanor was always able to read me. She fixed me with a penetrating stare. "Are you okay with that?"

I shrugged. "I had to come back to start classes and my job. I'm a floor counselor in Sulzberger."

"The freshman dorm at Barnard? Ugh!"

"I'm glad to have the money and a place to live." Tears burned behind my eyes. I was horrified I might start crying. I was feeling pretty discontented with my situation. For one thing, compared to our adventures in Luxor with ancient curses, Nile crocodiles, and antiquities smugglers, I was afraid life on an Ivy League campus would seem routine and tame. More important, I missed Cass like crazy, and I was feeling unsure and insecure about where our relationship was going and when we might be together again.

Eleanor picked up on my feelings. She covered my hand with hers.

I cleared my throat. "She writes me from Cairo every few days. She always signs her letters, 'All my love, Cass.'"

"That's encouraging."

"Yes, but I guess it's my nature to never be satisfied."

She nodded. "You and I share that trait."

I wasn't sure she and I meant the same thing about not being satisfied. For Eleanor, it meant serial affairs. On my part, I wanted to be sure of Cass's feelings for me.

Eleanor took off her sunglasses and looked into my eyes with a little smile. Her hand was warm on mine. "I've missed you, Ari.

You know you can come to my apartment anytime. Come tonight. We'll order take-out and catch up."

I was tempted. Eleanor has a posh apartment on the Upper East Side with an incredible view of the park. She scored it in one of her divorces. We had great times there last year, but I knew what "catch up" meant to Eleanor, and that would only complicate my personal life. Thankfully, an interruption saved me from making a bad decision.

"Dr. Frame. I thought we were meeting in the library." The young woman was tall with a bouncy ponytail that showed sun streaks, whether real or from a bottle—hard to tell. I had seen her around the Barnard campus, always at the head of a posse of girls who appeared to be going to or coming from some place important. I figured she must be Eleanor's pick for the semester.

Eleanor looked at her watch. "Of course, Abby. I was early and ran into Ari Morgan. You two must know each other. Have a seat and you can join us for a cup of coffee."

I stood up. "I'll be going, Dr. Frame. I need to get back to the dorm. We have tons of meetings before the start of school. Nice to see you, and you too, Abby."

Chapter Two

THE NEXT TWO WEEKS Sulzberger Hall was a madhouse with the last of the freshmen moving in the dorm, student registration, and classes starting. It rained hard every day of the first week. The whole place smelled of wet cardboard boxes, and dripping umbrellas created an obstacle course across the lobby. The ancient elevator gave up the ghost the first day, so we had to recruit boys from Columbia to carry suitcases up the steep stairs to the third and fourth floors.

By the third week, things had settled into a routine. My professor in Finer Elements of Creative Writing wasn't nearly as lame as I had feared. He was actually a fairly successful playwright and tried to keep the class interesting. He encouraged us to get things down on paper and worry about editing later. That was a different approach for me and a challenge in a good way. I was also taking a class in techniques of TV production, a nice break from writing.

From time to time, I saw Abby on campus. We exchanged head nods but didn't speak. She was never with Eleanor, but that was Dr. Frame's style. She avoided being seen in public with her latest.

Cass kept up writing chatty letters full of funny stories about her work in the basement laboratory of the Egyptian Museum and the petty politics among Egyptologists who were jealous of her accomplishments.

One Wednesday evening before the Christmas break, I found a package wrapped in brown paper in my cubbyhole in the dorm's office. It was postmarked Cairo with Cass's return address. I tore into the wrapping. Inside was a book written fifty years earlier by a guy named Ludwig Borchardt titled *Excavations at Tell el-Amarna*. On the cover, a grainy photograph showed eight white people sitting in folding camp chairs with palm trees and sand dunes in the background. They were dressed in formal Western clothes and comically huge pith helmets, trying to look relaxed but not succeeding.

A card with Cass's bold handwriting stuck out of the book. *Look at pages 36 and 37 and especially paragraph three on 37. I'll call you on Friday the 12th at eight o'clock your time after you've had a chance to look the book over.*

I ran up the stairs two at a time, the ancient elevator still out of service. I settled on my narrow bed and opened the book to page 36. It was a full-page black-and-white photograph of the famous bust of Nefertiti. The astonishing photo would have been even more so in color. I guessed Borchardt published the book before color photography was invented. If you've spent much time in ancient Egyptian tombs or museums you've seen stiff, stylized, two-dimensional figures always shown in profile. Nefertiti's bust was different. Even without the colors, the figure in the book was so lifelike you could swear she was about to speak, and the look on her face implied if she spoke she'd sound smart and a little sarcastic. The photo showed some damage to both ears, and her left eye was completely missing. Still, she was amazingly well preserved for an over three-thousand-year-old lady.

On the facing page, this Borchardt guy described finding the bust in 1912 in the ancient ruins of a sculptor's workshop in the royal city that King Akhenaten and Queen Nefertiti built in the desert.

In paragraph three, the one Cass told me to pay attention to, Borchardt wrote, "Immediately after we found the bust in Thutmose's workshop, I ordered a search for the missing inlay from the left eye. The debris, even that which we had already removed, was searched, and some of it sifted. We found a few more fragments of the ears, but not the eye inlay. Only much later did I realize the left eye had never existed. Thutmose did not mean the bust to be part of a larger statue or a worship piece in its own right. The left eye socket remains empty because he meant the piece to be a model. The artist had no purpose in repeating the eye which would have been a mirror image of the right inlay."

I flipped on my bedside lamp and held the photo under it. The artist had painted minute details on her crown and the wide floral collar around her neck. You could even make out individual hairs in her eyebrows. If the sculptor meant the bust for a model, he certainly went to great pains for realism. Borchardt concluded his account of finding the bust with, "She cannot be described, she must be seen."

I spent the next few days going back and forth across Broadway to classes at Columbia and wishing time would speed up. On Friday, I arranged and rearranged the clothes in my tiny closet twice, then at ten minutes before eight o'clock I staked out the stuffy public phone cubicle across from my door. The phone rang right on time. I grabbed it before the second ring. "Hello?"

"Hello. Is this a good time for you to talk?" The connection sounded tinny, but Cass's voice sent an electric tingle down my spine just the same. "I figured all your flock at Barnard would be down to dinner or getting ready for dates or something. Do you feel you have a foot in each camp working at Barnard and being in graduate school at Columbia?"

"I feel fortunate to have a job and a place to live while I'm in school. And it's a fine time to call. I'm glad to hear your voice. I miss you so much."

She made the familiar, sexy little chuckle that comes from her diaphragm. "I miss you too."

There was a long pause, and I thought I might have lost the connection. "Cass? Are you there?"

"I'm here."

"Is everything alright? You sound down."

"I had determined not to call you halfway around the world and cry on your shoulder, but here we are. The problem is, I'm bored rigid. I'm not meant to be stuck in a dark basement laboratory. Hatshepsut's in good hands now with the Egyptian people. We've accomplished our mission to solve the mystery of her actual existence. I can leave the job of poring over every inch of her life and afterlife to the museum staff."

I felt a surge of hope. "What do you plan to do? Are you coming back to Columbia?"

"That's why I'm calling. Did you get the book I sent?"

"Yes. I've seen pictures of Nefertiti's bust many times. You'd have to be living under a rock not to because it's so famous."

"And you read Borchardt's narrative about her eye?"

"The left eye he concludes never got made in the first place."

"What if he's mistaken? About the eye and about the statue being meant to serve as a model. She seems too detailed."

"I noticed that too."

"Borchardt found crudely sculpted and unpainted stone models in the ruins of the workshop, but none with the detail and quality of Nefertiti. What if Thutmose created the Queen's bust as a worship piece in its own right? Her eye might exist somewhere waiting for us to find it and restore her perfection. Imagine the impact that would make! Such a discovery would change the whole narrative about the origin and purpose of one of the world's most famous works of art."

"Borchardt says he searched for the missing eye in the ruins without success."

"The search he describes sounds careless. Dig techniques were not so precise in 1912. He was in a rush to steal her away to Germany. He wanted to impress his financial backer."

"You're saying he stole the statue?"

"He misrepresented its importance. Germany and Egypt had agreed to divide significant finds at Tell el-Amarna equally. In his inventory Borchardt identified her as 'a painted plaster bust of a princess.' Certainly he could see she was more important than that. He placed her deep in a box in a poorly lit chamber to fool the chief antiquities inspector and hide her significance. He wrote in his private notes, 'I want to save the bust for us.' Meaning the Germans."

"That seems very wrong."

"Anyone who plunders a site for personal gain is no better than a graverobber, whether it's for his own personal enrichment or prestige or for chauvinistic recognition of a country. The Egyptians contend Nefertiti was removed from their country under false pretenses. They want her back. I want to help them."

I recognized the passion and excitement rising in Cass's voice like when we began our search for Hatshepsut. "So you want to find an eye that may or may not have ever existed but in any case has been missing for three thousand years, restore the statue, and convince Germany to return her to Egypt?"

"That's one of the things I love about you, darling. Your brain works in such linear terms. One step at a time. You're right that finding the eye is first. About returning Nefertiti...if Borchardt cheated to get her, isn't it fair the Egyptian people have her back? It's certainly a quest that would spring me out of the basement of the Egyptian Museum. I yearn to be in the field again."

"How do you hope to find Nefertiti's eye?"

"I know where I'll start. In the Ägyptisches Museum in Berlin where Nefertiti's bust is now. Plus, I've found a clue."

"What clue?"

"It's too much to tell you on the phone." She paused again. "Meet me in Berlin."

I slid down the wall of the phone booth to sit cross-legged on the floor. "Meet you. In Berlin."

"Why not? You have the holiday break coming up. The Germans make a big to-do over Christmas. They decorate all the streets and gather in beautiful markets with colorful handmade gifts and mulled wine and special cakes. They invented Santa Claus, you know."

"They did?"

"I haven't done the research, but I think so. Anyway, we'll have a wonderful time."

"I don't know. This is so last minute. Mom and Gran are expecting me in Beaufort."

"I understand." She sounded really disappointed. "You wouldn't want to upset them." Her words seemed more like a question than a statement.

I chewed a hangnail. "No, I wouldn't do that for the world. I suppose I could call Mom and try out the idea. Maybe they wouldn't mind too much."

A girl, one of my flock, as Cass put it, appeared outside the phone cubicle and began pacing. I held up a finger.

Cass's end of the line crackled again. "Well, think it over. I'll hold off a week making my travel arrangements in case you can join me."

That sent the tingle down my back again. I fought an urge to yell, *Of course I'll come.* Instead, I said, "I'll let you know."

I hung up and checked for the girl waiting for the phone. She had given up. Meeting Cass in Berlin might be a great opportunity to move my relationship with her to the next level. I pictured Mom and Gran's house in Beaufort, North Carolina on Ann Street across from the United Methodist Church and the Old Burying Ground. They would be finishing up washing the supper dishes. This was as good a time as any to call. Mom answered on the second ring. "Hello?"

"Mom, it's Ari."

"I knew it was you, honey. I have a sixth sense about when you're calling. Are you all right?"

"I'm fine." I could hear the theme music from *Jeopardy* in the background. I pictured my grandmother in her favorite chair with her feet up in front of their twenty-year-old television. "Gran's watching her program."

"Yes, she doesn't miss it in the daytime, then she watches the reruns on the local channel at night. She's convinced if Art Fleming would let her on the show she'd win us a bushel basket of money."

I heard Gran's voice in the living room yelling at the TV. "Who is Zelda Fitzgerald?"

"But if she watches the rerun, doesn't she know the answers already?"

"She says that's a good thing about getting old. You forget."

Mom held her hand over the receiver. "Turn the TV set down, Mama. Ari's calling long distance from New York City." She came back on the line. "We're counting the days till you come home. The Boy Scouts delivered a spruce from the Christmas tree lot yesterday. They'll do that if you're old ladies like us. The tree's waiting for you in the living room. We'll decorate it when you're here. You have a good eye for how to make everything so pretty. Of course, Mama will whip up her famous homemade snow you like to put on the branches. She refuses to give me the recipe. It has something to do with Ivory Soap and cornstarch. I suppose owning a secret makes her feel important and an integral part of the whole thing, so we humor her, but..."

I took a deep breath and jumped in. "That's why I'm calling. Dr. Stillwell has asked me to travel to Berlin over the holidays. To help her investigate an ancient artifact. The bust of Nefertiti."

"Berlin, Germany?"

"Yes."

"Oh, then you'd be in Berlin, Germany on Christmas?" Her disappointment fairly jumped across the telephone lines.

"Yes, I told her you're expecting me in Beaufort. If you have lots of plans for us, I don't have to go to Germany. She has a theory that the Queen's missing eye exists someplace waiting to be discovered, and she wants me to help her." I felt guilty playing up the archaeological research aspect when I really just wanted to be with Cass, but I plunged ahead. "I told her you might feel disappointed."

I heard the rustle of the receiver changing hands. "Honey, you go ahead on your trip."

"Gran? Have you been eavesdropping?"

"You go ahead to Germany. Your mother and I have plenty to keep us busy this time of year. The activities at the church are nonstop, and you know the Garden Club always decorates a float for the Christmas Eve parade. Come home after the holidays when we have more time to visit." She dropped her voice. "This trip with Dr. Stillwell sounds special. She's so pretty and smart as a whip. I can tell from her interviews on the television. And famous. Why just yesterday there was a question on *Jeopardy* about Hatshepsut. You go ahead, honey. Do you know how excited your mother or I would have been at your age for the chance to go to Berlin, Germany with someone special?"

Mom took the phone back. She cleared her throat like she was trying to avoid tearing up. "Your gran is right. Go on your trip and come home in the spring. You remember how sweet the air smells with the magnolias in bloom. And bring Dr. Stillwell with you. Beaufort, North Carolina isn't as ancient as Egypt, but we do go back to 1713. That's old for the United States. We had Blackbeard the Pirate and all. She might find us interesting."

"Of course she would. I promise to come for spring break. Are you sure it's okay, Mom?"

"Just stay safe, honey."

"Thank you, Mom. I love you. Hug Gran for me."

"You hang up first."

She always says that. "I love you both."

Chapter Three

THE PLANE BOUNCED TWICE on its landing gear, then braked and settled into a steady taxi to our gate at Berlin Brandenburg Airport. The stewardess made a speech in German that I couldn't understand a bit of, but even if the words had been English I would have had trouble hearing over my heart beating in my ears from the anticipation of seeing Cass. Judging from the rest of the passengers, the announcement signaled it was okay to gather your stuff and head for the exit. Going down the portable stairs to the tarmac, I shaded my eyes and scanned the windows in the terminal for Cass. She was standing there, smiling and waving. My heartbeat got even faster if possible.

Inside the terminal, holiday travelers crowded the concourse, herding children and juggling luggage, checking flight information, and talking fast in German. The PA system blared out familiar melodies of Christmas carols. Cass and I navigated toward each other through the throng. She held my shoulders and looked me up and down. "You look good. The same."

"It's been only a few months." I said this as a cover-up for how excited I was to see her.

"I know, but it seems longer. Thank you for coming." She hugged me tight. You know how sometimes when you embrace someone the fit is perfect? That's how hugging Cass feels. We stood entwined for a while with people swirling around us.

"Good." She picked up my bag. "The hotel's in the Charlottenburg district near the museum where the bust is. I've been here two days already, so I'm all settled. I've held off going to the museum to see Nefertiti until you got here." She draped an arm around my shoulders, and we started down the concourse. "How was the flight? Are you very tired? You can sleep in tomorrow and recover from any jet lag. We'll go to the museum in the early afternoon."

"I should feel tired, but it's the opposite. I think it's an adrenaline rush from seeing you." Why deny it?

She whispered in my ear. "Let's hurry, then, so we can be alone and catch up." I hoped she meant what I thought she did. Cass hailed a taxi and gave the driver the address. She held my hand and pointed out landmarks along the route from south to north through the middle of Berlin. I expected to see sad bombed-out buildings with bullet holes in the walls like in the old black and white newsreels of the Allied forces marching into the city at the end of the war. Instead, modern high-rise buildings lined neat, wide boulevards busy with rush hour traffic. Pedestrians clogged the sidewalks. No sign of the war that killed over five million Germans.

Cass had picked a boutique hotel in a quiet residential suburb near Charlottenburg Palace, with Nefertiti's museum across the street. The small lobby of the hotel was unoccupied except for a distinguished-looking middle-aged man relaxing in front of a fireplace with his legs crossed reading the newspaper. He had a mustache and close-cropped gunmetal gray hair.

You can tell a lot about a person by their shoes. He wore oxford lace-ups. They were conservative and expensive looking and probably handmade. He glanced at us and went back to his paper.

We followed the bellman to the elevator. Cass kept smiling at me, which didn't do anything to calm my nerves. Our room was on the top level with a view of the palace from floor-to-ceiling windows. The palace courtyard sparkled with hundreds of colored lights. A massive Ferris wheel towered over rows of tents. "Cass, I think that's a Christmas market at the palace. Can we go?"

"We'll go tomorrow night. Christmas Eve in the market will be special."

I followed the bellman around the room while he explained everything in German, which again I didn't understand a word of. I just kept nodding. Cass tipped him, and finally he was gone and we were alone. As soon as the door latch clicked, we fell into each other's arms and started kissing and shedding clothes till we were both naked.

I broke away. "Take a shower with me first. I smell like airplane."

"Huh-uh. Can't wait." She guided me backward onto the bed, and I sank into a goose down comforter. She straddled me and began a rocking motion while she explored my nipples with her mouth. The gold necklace she always wears dangled between her breasts and swayed in time with the friction between our bodies. The necklace is Hatshepsut's cartouche. In the center of the charm the Queen is seated on a throne holding a diamond in her outstretched hands. The clarity of the stone as it caught sunlight streaming in the windows was remarkable. I'm no expert, but the charm looks really expensive.

The necklace made me think of the woman who gave it to Cass, Dr. Jessie Finn Markham, her professor at Oxford. She died of breast cancer two years ago. Cass told me their relationship was never physical but somehow deeper than that. The woman was Cass's mentor. She taught Cass their profession shouldn't be about digging up pottery shards for the glory of a particular country but rather the unity of the past and present with lessons for all people.

I tried imagining how I would ever compete with Cass's pure-as-the-driven-snow feelings for a dead woman who could afford to give her expensive gifts. All the thinking was distracting me. I arched into her thrusts and the heat between our bodies. She let out a gasp and climaxed. She rolled off me and lay with her eyes closed, breathing through her mouth.

When she recovered normal breathing she said, "Lovely," then rolled on her side and began tracing a path of kisses up the insides of my thighs. That took care of all the distraction.

* * * * *

The Berlin Ägyptisches Museum is in the restored House of the Royal Guards, across the road from Charlottenburg Palace. I was surprised how modest the building looked. The museum housed the most famous Egyptian relic ever except for maybe Tutankhamun's gold mask, but by its appearance, the building could be a courthouse on the square in any southern American county seat. The place looked closed, and there was a sign in German on the door.

"What does the sign say?"

Cass rang the bell. "It says the museum is closed for the day to accommodate a special event. That's us. The Minister for Arts and Antiquities has been very cooperative."

"He knows you're famous for finding Hatshepsut."

"Whatever, he's allowing us access to Nefertiti up close without the distraction of other visitors."

We heard scurrying footsteps inside and the scratch of the dead bolt. A female attendant in a black uniform with a white lace collar opened the door halfway. "Ja?"

"I'm Dr. Cassandra Stillwell and this is Ariadne Morgan."

The attendant didn't move.

"Minister Lothar Stoph."

That did the trick. The attendant swung the door open and indicated we should follow her across the lobby and up some stairs to the second level. She pointed to the room on the right. Statues of reclining figures with lions' bodies and rams' heads lined the gallery. At the end of the walkway Nefertiti's bust rested inside a glass cube on a pedestal. Cass gasped and put her hand to her mouth.

A voice from behind us said, "She's astonishing, is she not?" We whirled around to face as physically imposing a woman as you'll ever run across. She was about six feet tall with broad shoulders, platinum-blond hair—the real thing, not out of a bottle—and icy blue eyes. "It is as her discoverer Borchardt said, 'She cannot be described. She must be seen.'" The woman stepped forward, offered Cass her hand, and made a little bow. I think she clicked her heels too. "Dr. Stillwell, Helga von Halle, Vice Minister of Arts and Antiquities. The Minister has asked I provide any assistance you require." She stepped back and stood at attention waiting for Cass's response.

Cass suppressed a little smile and cleared her throat. "Excellent. Meet my assistant, Ariadne Morgan. She'll be taking notes of our observations." She glanced down the gallery at Nefertiti. "Well, shall we take a look?"

"Certainly." Helga led the way down the row of lion-rams till we stood in front of the bust. She took a pair of white gloves from her jacket pocket and lifted the glass enclosure covering the Queen. I fumbled in my bag for a spiral notebook and pen and waited for Cass to make the next move.

She took a deep, shuddering breath. "Overwhelming." Then the analytical scientist part of Cass's personality kicked in. She made one slow, complete circle around the bust. She began to dictate. "The work represents the upper part of the Queen, her head, neck, and an area extending downward from the clavicle to just above the breasts. She wears a tall crown painted dark blue. Her head appears hairless beneath the crown. The preservation is astoundingly good. Some damage to both ears and the sharp upper edge of the crown, but she's remarkably intact. The colors are as vibrant as though they were painted yesterday."

I scrambled to keep up with notes of her observations.

Cass leaned closer to the bust. "Symmetrical eye sockets rimmed with black kohl. The left eye socket is empty. No obvious traces of glue in the empty eye, but the inside is painted white, matching the right eye. Pink-brown skin tone overall with deeper red-brown lips and dark eyebrows."

Helga interrupted. "With your permission, Dr. Stillwell, may I ask what you deduce from the light skin tone? Some have proposed she was Aryan. Do you think she could have been a foreign-born queen?"

Cass hesitated before responding. I saw a familiar glint in her eye. She was turning her analytical high beams on Helga von Halle. "It's commonly believed she was born in Thebes. She certainly grew up there in the palace. I'm not sure we can make any assumption from the skin color Thutmose chose. He may have followed color conventions that decreed elite men were depicted with red-brown skin and women with paler yellow-white."

Helga didn't seem convinced. "Ah. One of several mysteries then, such as whether her left eye ever existed."

"Yes. Will you tilt the bust so I can see the underside?"

"Of course." Helga carefully tipped the statue backward to expose the bottom. I squinted to try and see what Cass was looking for. The bottom was a flat unpainted surface.

"The base is flat white limestone, the surface somewhat uneven as one would expect in an authentic piece since the tops of ancient wooden work tables would have been irregular."

Cass took a step backward. She stood still for a moment with her eyes closed as though communing with Nefertiti like the first time I saw her in the Museum of Modern Art with Hatshepsut's statue. She turned to Helga. "Thank you for your assistance, and please give my regards to Minister Stoph. He was kind to accommodate us today." She looked around the gallery. "I'm feeling a bit guilty having deprived visitors of seeing Nefertiti. I suspect hundreds fill the gallery every hour of every day."

Helga followed her gaze. "Yes, hundreds come and half are turned away because of the modest size of Ägyptisches Museum. Such a remarkable artifact deserves better. She has not always been here. If you have finished your examination, you might be interested in seeing her true home."

"Of course."

Helga carefully replaced the glass case over the bust and led us outside to a black Mercedes sedan parked in front of the museum. She held the back door open for us, gave instructions to the driver, and climbed in the front seat. We drove east past crowds of last-minute Christmas shoppers on boulevards decorated for the holidays. Helga kept up a proud running commentary about the parks and monuments and other landmarks we passed. She turned to face us. "Soon we will reach the demarcation between West and East Berlin. The border guards may retain your passports. Do not be concerned. They will return your documents when we cross back over."

In the middle of the boulevard, a sign announced, "You are leaving the American Sector," then repeated the warning in Russian and French. Ahead the Berlin Wall separated the Allied forces' West Berlin from Soviet East Berlin. Our driver stopped beside a kiosk, and Helga rolled down her window. A soldier in a drab green wool Soviet uniform with a rifle slung over his shoulder bent to check out everyone in the car. Helga flashed an ID, and the guard said something in Russian. "He's requesting your passports." Cass handed hers through the front window. The soldier looked at the picture, then studied her face and said in English, "British? What is your business in the Soviet Sector?"

Helga answered before Cass could speak. "Dr. Stillwell is a distinguished archaeologist and scholar from Columbia University in New York City. She and her assistant, Miss Morgan, are visiting Berlin to study ancient artifacts."

He looked at me. "Passport."

I handed mine over, and he checked the picture and said, "American" like he had a bad taste in his mouth and needed to spit. He stuck the passports in his inside pocket and waved us through.

I whispered to Cass. "Are you sure that's okay?"

Cass squeezed my hand and shook her head to shush me. Unlike West Berlin, East Berlin was the post-war city I expected from old newsreels. The gloomy streets reminded me of the movie *The Wizard of Oz,* where the beginning of the film in Kansas, before the tornado, was shot in gray sepia tones. Once Dorothy lands in Oz, everything is brilliant Technicolor. Except Berlin was the exact opposite. We drove from the bright, prosperous American sector of the city into a drab gray landscape on the Soviet side. Every third or fourth building had been bombed by the Allies at the end of the war and never replaced. The few people on the sidewalks shuffled along with their heads down. Even the sky seemed overcast just across the demarcation line.

The driver stopped at the curb in front of a ruined building. What remained of the structure looked like the prow of an art deco ship. Helga climbed out and opened our door. She led us across a dilapidated walkway that didn't look entirely safe. I held my breath till we made our way to the other side. "This area was called Museum Island before the war. The Neues Museum, you see what's left of it, was Nefertiti's home from 1924 until 1939. She had her own courtyard all to herself in a wonderful opulent building."

She led us inside a massive entry gallery with the ruined roof open to the sky and a giant round bomb hole in the middle of the marble mosaic floor. Cass took my arm. "Watch your step."

Helga pointed to the remains of two sweeping curved staircases that once led to the second level. Trees grew where the steps would have been. "In August of 1939, Berlin's museums were forced to close in anticipation of enemy bombs. The authorities packed up the collections and transferred them to secure locations. As you can see, that was a wise decision. More than a third of the Neues Museum was destroyed."

I piped up. "And the Germans have not rebuilt it in over thirty years since."

Helga drew herself up to her full six feet. "Your countries divided our homeland after the war." Her voice shook with emotion. She was fighting to weigh her words and losing the battle. "Someday, the Wall will come down. The German people will be one again. Then Nefertiti's home can be restored."

A cloud passed over the sun and three blackbirds rose squawking from the top of one of the trees. Cass waited till the birds' calls died away. "What of the Egyptian claim that Borchardt took Nefertiti under false pretenses?"

Helga's blue eyes turned even icier. "We are fully aware of the public debate about the value of restitution. We can ponder whether the British Museum should return the Rosetta Stone or the Louvre give the Mona Lisa back to Italy, but what of the value a great museum offers the citizens of every nation, not only of one? Someday the German people will restore Neues Museum as the magnificent institution it was before the war for all the world to appreciate, and Nefertiti will be back where she belongs." She turned and headed toward the car. "Let us retrieve your passports."

Cass shot me a raised-eyebrow look.

Chapter Four

IT WAS DUSK WHEN Helga's Mercedes dropped us in front of our hotel. Noise from the Christmas market drifted across the boulevard. We watched the giant Ferris wheel make a slow turn over the tops of vendor tents. Cass ran her fingers through her hair. "Let's freshen up and go to the market. There'll be plenty of choices for food. We can make it our dinner."

I looked for the man with the expensive shoes in the lobby, but the chairs around the fireplace were empty. Upstairs, I sat on the foot of the bed and opened my notebook. "What did you learn from inspecting the bust? I want to make sure I got all your observations in my notes."

"She's genuine, not a fake as some have suggested. I understand skeptics questioning her authenticity. Busts from that period are very rare. Artists almost always painted or sculpted the whole figure, from head to toe, because they believed if anything happened to the mummy, the spirit could occupy the painted or sculpted image into the afterlife. Nobody wanted to be stuck in eternity as a head without a body. But other busts have been found. They're usually in ruins of royal living quarters."

I wrote that tidbit in my notes. "She appears so modern, too. Like our contemporary idea of beauty. She looks like Audrey Hepburn."

Cass laughed. "She does. You're right."

"Helga's question about the skin color being Aryan was weird. Her words sounded more like an assertion than a question. If you want to repatriate Nefertiti, it may have to be over Helga's dead body."

"Yes. I noticed."

"Are you going to tell me about the clue you've found that started this quest?"

Cass rubbed her hands together. "Ah." She opened her briefcase, took out a file folder, and sat beside me on the bed. "This is a rather long story. Are you terribly hungry?"

"No, I can wait." I leaned back on my elbows.

Cass opened the folder. "In the early 1900s, a wealthy American industrialist named Theodore M. Davis conducted many successful digs in the Valley of the Kings across the river from the ancient city of Thebes, known as Luxor today. Over the course of twelve years, he opened thirty tombs."

"Wow. More than two a year."

"Yes. In 1907 he discovered KV55, a tomb containing the coffin and mummy of King Akhenaten. For context, the KV55 discovery happened five years before Borchardt unearthed Nefertiti's bust and fifteen years before Carter found Tutankhamen's tomb."

"It sounds like an important discovery."

She nodded. "King Akhenaten's original royal tomb had been found several years earlier at Tell el-Amarna almost three hundred miles north, but the burial chamber was empty. Egyptologists assumed robbers broke into the tomb in antiquity and stole or destroyed the mummy. With Davis's discovery, the world learned the King's true fate. At some point in ancient history his mummy was moved back to Thebes, the imperial city he had abandoned in favor of a new royal city in the desert."

"So King Akhenaten's mummy is the clue to Nefertiti's eye?"

"Indirectly. Bear with me. Mr. Davis always traveled with his live-in mistress, Emma Andrews. Emma made herself useful during his digs by carefully recording his discoveries and keeping an inventory of all the antiquities removed and transported to the Egyptian Museum in Cairo. She was also an inveterate diarist her whole life. When she died in 1922, she left all her papers including her diaries to the Cairo Museum. Here's where the clue to Nefertiti's eye comes in. A month ago I was exploring the archives in the basement of the museum, and I found Emma Andrews's diary describing the discovery of KV55 and her meticulous inventory of the items Davis found."

"You were bored and just poking around."

"Exactly. In the diary I came across this." She handed me a Xerox of a page with a sketch of a tomb drawing. Underneath the picture handwritten in fancy script the way they used to learn to write was the legend: "Tomb painting on the burial chamber wall of KV55. The only such painting in the entire tomb."

The sketch showed two male figures. The one on the left was wrapped like a mummy. He wore a king's crown and held a flail and crook. The figure on the right was a youth of twelve or so. He knelt on one knee and offered the mummy king a small box as a tribute. Above the two figures, the round disk of Aten the sun god radiated beams of light. Each beam terminated in a human hand or an ankh. One beam was different. It pointed straight down and ended in a left eye lined in black kohl, a match to the right one on Nefertiti's bust.

Cass pointed to the hieroglyphs along the side. "This is King Akhenaten's royal name cartouche. The rest says, 'Praise to King Akhenaten and his Great Wife Nefertiti from Thutmose the Sculptor, Favorite of the King.'"

"Who is the boy?"

"There's no indication. He appears too young to be Thutmose. The sculptor would have worn elaborate robes. The boy is dressed in the loincloth of a worker. Whoever he is, I think this painting shows Nefertiti's eye is in the small chest the boy is offering to the dead king. I believe the eye is almost certainly in KV55."

I looked at the sketch again. "You say the eye is still in the tomb? Davis didn't find it?"

"Emma kept meticulous inventories of Davis's many finds, no matter how seemingly insignificant, down to individual beads from unstrung necklaces. I'm convinced if they had found the eye in the chest, she would have noted it."

"And even if they had found the chest, Davis and Emma would have thought the relic was some random crystal eyeball. They wouldn't have understood its importance because the bust would not be found for another five years."

Cass nodded. "Yes, and to complicate matters further, Borchardt kept the bust a secret for ten years after his discovery. The first public announcement of her existence was in 1923, and both Davis and Emma were dead by then."

I pictured my hope that Cass would come back to New York and take up her professorship at Columbia blowing away like the shifting sands of the Sahara Desert. "You plan to open KV55 and search for the eye."

"Yes. Davis resealed the tomb in 1909. It hasn't been entered since. Alfi is meeting with the Egyptian Ministry of Antiquities to secure permits."

Alfi is Cass's dig lieutenant when she's in Egypt. He's very competent, so no use counting on some kind of problem with Cass getting the permits.

She pushed up from the bed. "As soon as I return to Luxor we'll start putting together the expedition. Now let's go have some fun at the market."

Two life-sized angels stood guard on either side of the entrance to the Christmas fair. Inside the gates the crowd noise competed with a brass quartet playing "Oh, Tannenbaum." The giant Ferris wheel towered over rows of festively decorated wooden huts and canvas tents.

Cass pulled me close to her side. "Are you warm enough?" She pointed to a brightly lit tent. "Let's get a mulled wine to take off the chill before we explore the booths."

"I'm game, but what's mulled wine?"

"Half red wine, half brandy, heated with spices. You'll like the taste but be careful. The alcohol sneaks up on you."

The drink came in a souvenir ceramic cup with a picture of the palace on it. "Do we get to keep these?"

Cass laughed. "Yes."

The mulled wine was delicious, steaming hot and infused with cloves and cinnamon. She was right. I did like the taste, and I felt a little lightheaded after only a few sips. Smells of gingerbread, candied apples, and freshly baked loaves warm out of wood-fired ovens followed us down rows of merchant stalls offering Christmas lights, tree decorations, and nativity figures.

We passed a food stall that smelled like toasted cheese. "What's that?"

Cass stepped up to the counterman. "It's called raclette. Let's have some." She held up two fingers. "Zwei."

The man cut a wheel of swiss cheese into two semicircles and positioned one half under an open flame. When the cheese was melted and toasty, he scraped generous helpings onto two thick slices of fresh-baked bread and passed them over the counter. While Cass paid I surveyed the crowd. I noticed the man with the expensive shoes from the hotel lobby inspecting Christmas ornaments at a booth down the way behind us. He bought one and stuck the little package in his coat pocket.

Cass and I strolled along the line of vendors eating our delicious raclette and dodging oncoming traffic. I stopped at a booth that sold miniature balsa wood whirly-gig tree ornaments crafted in the Black Forest. When you held the ornament up and blew on it just right, tiny Mary, Joseph, Baby Jesus, and the manger animals danced around a Christmas tree. "I'm buying this for Mom and Gran."

Cass's gaze focused on me like she was probing my mind. "It's Christmas Eve. Are you disappointed you're not in Beaufort with them?"

I looked at my watch. "Two p.m. in North Carolina. The parade down Main Street is just stepping off. Mom and Gran always march with the Garden Club. I miss them, and I know they're missing me, but I'm glad to be here with you."

Cass hugged me. Over her shoulder I saw the man from the hotel lobby again. "Cass, did you notice a man in our hotel lobby when you brought me from the airport? Sitting by the fire reading a newspaper."

She nodded. "The one with the bespoke shoes."

"Bespoke?"

"Handmade."

"Yes. So you noticed him."

"I did, and he's been following us since we arrived at the market."

"Why didn't you say something? Who is he?"

"I don't know. Maybe one of Helga's colleagues. You registered her assertion about the statue's skin color and her strong reaction when I mentioned the Egyptian claim that Borchardt took Nefertiti under false pretenses. As you said, she suspects our motives in studying the bust." She glanced at the shoe man. He had stopped to buy some mulled wine. "Never mind him. He seems harmless."

"You're not concerned about being followed?"

"He probably has orders to track our whereabouts." Cass took my arm. "But enough unpleasant talk for the night. We'll ignore him. Let's not let him spoil our evening. We have several more days to enjoy the sights in Berlin before we get back to business."

I wasn't so sure we should ignore being followed and spied on.

She pointed to the Ferris wheel. "How about a ride?" She poked me in the ribs. "Maybe they'll stop us at the top and I can steal a kiss."

* * * * *

It was after midnight when Cass opened our hotel room door and let me go in first. We fell exhausted into bed. Cass flipped on the bedside lamp to read for a while. She looked adorable with her reading glasses perched on the end of her nose. I was dozing off when I noticed a shadow break the strip of light underneath the door leading into our room from the hallway. An envelope slid under the door. I propped up on one elbow. "What was that?"

"What?"

"Someone slipped an envelope under our door."

"Probably something from the hotel. It'll wait till morning." She kissed me and went back to her book.

The next morning, I got up to go to the bathroom and accidently kicked the envelope halfway across the carpet. I picked it up and turned it over. "Cass?"

She stretched and yawned. "I stayed awake too late reading."

"Cass, does the hotel have a logo that's a blood-red background behind an evil-looking black bird?"

"Of course not. What do you mean?"

I handed her the envelope.

She examined the logo on the outside of the white envelope. "Interesting." She opened the letter and read to herself. "Ari, call the front desk and ask if anyone inquired for our room number last evening."

"What does the letter say?"

"Call downstairs now please." She went to the window and closed the drapes.

I picked up the bedside phone and dialed.

The clerk answered on the first ring. "How may I be of assistance?"

"This is Dr. Stillwell's room. Did anyone ask for our room number last evening?"

"No, madam."

I hung up and shook my head. "No one asked. You're scaring me. What does the letter say?"

She sat on the bed and read from the paper. "Dr. Stillwell, your contempt for your profession's established order is well known. Now you hope to use the Nefertiti bust as the next step to burnish your reputation. We will stand in your way on behalf of all

Aryans. The temporary setback that resulted in our country's disunity will soon be rectified. Germany will emerge in all her dignity, pride, and grandeur. The artifact will return to her rightful place in a world-renowned museum. She belongs to our people. We will not allow you to diminish our racial and cultural superiority."

I felt a tingle of fear in my chest. I dropped on the bed beside Cass. "They're calling World War Two a temporary setback? Who's it from?"

"No signature, of course. Cowards."

"What about the logo? Is that a clue?"

She turned the envelope over and ran her thumb across the image. "The bird is a phoenix. In ancient Egypt the image symbolized immortality, resurrection, and life after death. This is the flag of the National Identity Underground. They're a group of leftovers from Hitler Youth after the end of the war. They're middle-aged now but still stuck in what they would call the glory days of the Third Reich."

"Helga could have written that letter. The part about Germany reunifying and emerging with pride are almost the same words she used at the ruined museum."

Cass nodded. "She was a little more subtle, but not much. She's about the right age." She went back to reading the letter. "If you value your safety and that of those around you, terminate your mission and leave Berlin immediately."

She deliberately folded the paper and put it back in the envelope. Her face was flushed, and her lips pressed together in the tight straight line. I had seen that look before when we were hunting Hatshepsut. Fierce determination.

"The man who was following us at the market left the letter, didn't he? What are you going to do?"

"We're departing Berlin. Our business here is done anyway." She retrieved her suitcase from the closet and began emptying drawers. "You're going back to New York, and I'm going back to Cairo and on to Luxor to meet Alfi and get the KV55 dig started."

Cass went into the bathroom to collect her toothbrush and things, and I followed her. "But they said terminate your mission. Doesn't the threat mean they'll follow you to Egypt to stop you?"

"Pack your bag, Ari." She checked her watch. "I'll call the airport to change our flights."

I tailed her back into the bedroom. "I don't understand why you insist on putting yourself in harm's way. Her eye's been missing for three thousand years. What difference will a few more make?" My voice caught. I felt like crying from frustration.

She touched the charm on the chain around her neck like she was connecting with her love who died. "How can I preach against greed and nationalism in archaeology and run scared from a bunch of thugs' threats?"

"Well, I'm not going back to New York. I'm going with you to KV55."

"Don't be ridiculous. You have school and your job."

"You can get the dean to approve an independent study semester for me, and people will be standing in line to get my dorm job."

She took me by the shoulders. "Let's not waste time arguing. You heard the threat against those close to me. I'll have my hands full without worrying about your safety."

"Are you forgetting I've been questioned as a murder suspect and been shot at, let alone that I dove into crocodile-infested waters to retrieve Hatshepsut's crystal? I can take care of myself, and I can help you. You're not always aware of the danger you're in. Like now, you don't seem to be taking these threats seriously."

She slammed shut the suitcase lid with more force than necessary, ending the conversation. "I'll be better able to control things back in Egypt." She picked up the phone to call the airlines. "Now please get packed as I asked you."

Chapter Five

THE FIRST-CLASS LOUNGE at the airport was practically deserted. The uniformed attendant at the front desk checked our passports and tickets. "Welcome, Dr. Stillwell and Miss Morgan. As you see, you'll have your choice of seating here in the lounge. Christmas Day is our quietest time. Everyone has arrived at their destination, and they won't take return flights until tomorrow." She picked up the phone. "Find a spot and I'll check your flight status."

Cass chose overstuffed upholstered chairs beside a glass wall with a view of planes landing and taking off. The attendant walked up. "Dr. Stillwell, your Cairo flight connecting to Luxor shows an on-time departure. It's boarding in twenty minutes. Miss Morgan's JFK nonstop boards in two hours."

"Thanks."

"My pleasure."

I watched her walk back to the front desk. "She's certainly giving us a lot of special attention."

"Bored, most likely. Do you want some coffee or a roll? We didn't take time for breakfast. I'll watch your bag."

I shook my head. "I should be going with you."

She leaned in and kissed my cheek. "Darling, we've talked through the reason. Let's not part on a bad note. I must go now and find my gate. They'll call boarding for your flight here in the lounge, but pay attention. Sometimes things change, though the Germans have a reputation for keeping a schedule."

She looked around the deserted room. "You'll be all right here. Don't leave the lounge until they call your flight." Did Cass perceive more danger than she was letting on? "In Luxor I'll stay at the Winter Palace Hotel. I'll call you in New York when I'm settled." She gave me another one of those long perfect-fit hugs, picked up her bag, and headed for the exit. She stopped at the front desk and spoke to the attendant. Something about keeping an eye on me I figured. The woman glanced in my direction and nodded. Cass gave me a little wave and went out the door.

I watched a plane lumber down the auxiliary runway to line up for takeoff. They always seem so clumsy on the ground. I have to admit you wouldn't call me a great flier. I have this recurring nightmare. I'm on a plane and it taxis to take off and can't get up in the air so the pilot comes on the PA and says the plan has changed and we're going to drive all the way to our destination. Weird, huh?

I was still clutching my passport and ticket in my sweaty palm thinking I should go to Luxor with Cass. I could at least check the flights and see if there was a way to follow her. I pushed up from the chair and went to the front desk. The attendant smiled. "May I help you, Miss Morgan?"

"If I wanted to change my destination from New York to Luxor, would that be possible?"

"I can certainly check for you." She pulled out a thick catalogue of flights the size of the phone book. "What would you like me to explore?"

"Can I change my ticket, and when could I get there?"

She opened the book, licked her finger, and flipped through the tissue-paper-thin pages. "Let's see. You just missed the Cairo flight, of course. The next flight is nonstop at three o'clock, arriving at seven."

"Perfect."

"Oh, my."

"What?"

"The connection from Cairo to Luxor. You'll miss the only one of the day. The next one leaves twenty-four hours later. You'd be waiting in the airport for ages."

"Is there another way to get from Cairo to Luxor? What about a train?"

"That I can't help you with."

I paused a moment to make a quick mental pros and cons list. *Cons: First, Cass is likely to be really angry. Second, I'm not sure how I'll get to Luxor from Cairo. Third, I don't have much money, a little less than a hundred dollars. Fourth, there really could be danger waiting at KV55. Which brings up pros: In case of real danger, I'll be there to help Cass.* "And second, maybe we'll find the Queen's eye."

"I beg your pardon?"

I handed her my ticket and passport. "I'll take my chances. Can you book me on the three o'clock to Cairo?"

"Of course."

* * * * *

From Cairo Airport I took a taxi to Ramses Train Station in the city center. The driver dropped me in front of the colossal statue of Ramses II looming over the front entrance. Unlike the Berlin airport lounge, the inside of the art deco concourse was wall-to-wall people. Christmas Night was business as usual in the primarily Muslim country. I figured New York's Grand Central Station would look the same during Ramadan.

Crowd noise reverberated off the high ceiling and filled the space. People waited in long lines in front of the ticket counters lugging what appeared to be all their worldly possessions. I picked a line and spent the waiting time whispering phrases from my English to Arabic pocket dictionary for how to pay the fare to Luxor. That got me lots of curious looks. When I finally reached the front I was still fumbling with my bag and dictionary. The ticket clerk gave me an impatient look over the top of her glasses. "How may I help you, madam."

"Oh. You speak English. Great. The next train to Luxor."

"Second class or sleeper?"

My stomach growled from a combination of nerves and lack of food. "Sorry. How long is the trip?"

She glanced past me at the line of people waiting their turn. "The trip is about twelve hours, Madam."

I pictured the slim stack of bills in my wallet. "How much for the sleeper?"

She sighed. "Seventeen pounds."

I did some quick math. Forty American dollars. "Sleeper."

She handed me a ticket. "You must hurry. Track eleven."

The line of train cars on track eleven looked straight out of *Murder on the Orient Express.* The antique engine blew out a whooshing cloud of steam. I checked my ticket for a clue to the location of sleeper class. The ticket was in Arabic. Behind the engine, porters loaded a baggage car. Next came four cars with big yellow *2s* painted on the sides, packed with passengers, even a few standing in the aisles—I figured second class. Next came a dining car. Through the windows I could see tables covered with white cloths. At the very end of the train was a caboose. So the lone coach between the dining car and caboose must be the sleeper. How was that for detective work?

A conductor tweeted his whistle to signal final boarding, and a porter took my bag and helped me up the sleeper car's metal steps leading to a narrow hallway with a line of doors into small staterooms. Mine was halfway down. The interior of the stateroom was from a past era. The carpet was worn threadbare, a miniature sink supplied only a trickle of water, and the security chain on the door was broken. If Cass were here she'd say, "It's clean, and it'll get us where we're going."

I had barely gotten settled when the train lurched ahead. We were leaving on time. A good sign. We rattled south along the Nile through the Cairo suburbs and past the great pyramids of Giza silhouetted against the moon. There was a knock on the stateroom door. "Yes? Just a minute." I fumbled for my dictionary and opened the door.

It was the conductor. "Ticket, please." He inspected my ticket, punched it, and handed it back.

My stomach rumbled again. "Sorry. Is the dining car open?" I pantomimed raising a fork to my mouth in case he had reached the limit of his English.

"Yes, madam." He pointed up the hallway. "Next car forward."

I duck-walked along the narrow hallway against the swaying motion of the old coach and opened the sliding door at the end of the car. The rumbling noise of wheels on the tracks and a cold blast of air rushed in the open doorway. The maître d' seated me in the dining car at a small table with a white tablecloth, draped a napkin in my lap with a flourish, and placed a menu in front of me. Thank goodness it had English subtitles.

I ordered a green salad, soup, a roll with butter, and a glass of white wine. Egyptians grow fantastic lettuce and tomatoes. The delicious salad brought up a memory of the special dinner Cass and I shared on our balcony at the Winter Palace Hotel the night we first made love six months before. I was savoring the salad and the vision of Cass's incredible breasts when the sudden roar of the tracks caught my attention. Someone had opened the door at the back of the dining car. I turned and saw a bearded man holding open the door. His long cotton robe snapped around his ankles in the rush of wind. While I watched he turned toward me and gave an oddly piercing look, then disappeared into the darkness outside the car. Was that creepy or was I being paranoid? Did he have some connection with the warning letter Cass got in Berlin?

I finished my dinner and wine and went back to the sleeper car. No sign of the guy in the robe. Because the security chain inside my stateroom didn't work, I propped my suitcase against the door. Not that the case would stop someone who really wanted in, but having a barrier there made me feel better. I crawled in my bunk fully clothed and spent the longest night of my life. You would think the swaying motion of the train might be soothing like being rocked in a cradle, but every jerk felt like a minor earthquake. I slept in fits and finally gave up as the sky turned light enough for me to make out the date palms lining the riverbank beside the railroad tracks.

I opened Ludwig Borchardt's book and settled back to learn more about his Thutmose workshop dig. There came a door knock so faint I wasn't sure at first I'd really heard it. I waited, and the sound came a second time. "Yes?"

"Ticket, please."

Again? "Just a minute." I moved my suitcase aside and opened the door. The man in the cotton robe who gave me the fishy look was standing there pointing a gun at my heart. The muzzle looked as big as a cannon. I gasped and reflexively stepped backward, stumbling over the suitcase. He snatched me to my feet, poked the gun in the small of my back, and forced me out the door into the hallway. He shoved me toward the back of the car leading to the caboose.

This all happened within a few seconds, but the scene seemed to play out in slow motion. A hundred thoughts crowded my brain at the same time. *Should I yell for help? He's not that big. He's about my height. He did seem strong when he jerked me up off the floor, but maybe I could take him if I spun around. But a quick move would startle him, and he might jerk the trigger. Should I pull the emergency braking cord? Would a sudden stop throw him forward onto to me or toss me backward onto him? I should have paid better attention in high school physics class. Whichever, the force might cause him to pull the trigger.*

While these thoughts were spooling through my mind, he let out a surprised grunt and staggered backward. The gun flew out of his hand. I whirled to see another man with his arm around my assailant's neck. He was the man who followed Cass and me at the Christmas market in Berlin! The two fell to the floor and grappled in the narrow space, first one on top and then the other.

The guy in the robe broke away, snatched up the gun, and made for the door leading to the caboose. The other guy caught up with him, and they both plunged through the opening into the darkness outside. I heard a shout, a mix of surprise and fear, then silence. I stood plastered against the wall frozen with my mouth open. The Berlin guy came back through the door, smoothing his hair and straightening his tie. He brushed past me without a word and exited through the opposite end of the car.

I ran inside my stateroom and slammed the door, frantically looking around for a defensive weapon. I grabbed a ballpoint pen. Lame, but the only thing at hand. I propped the suitcase against the door and sat on the floor with my back braced against it. I wasn't looking forward to telling Cass what had happened. So much for my boast that I could take care of myself. If the Berlin guy hadn't intervened, who knows what the man in the robe had in mind for me? And was the Berlin guy saving me, or was the fight over who got the privilege of doing me in?

While I was mentally composing my narrative to Cass, the train slowed. The landscape began to change from rural patches of farmland to scatterings of country houses to tightly packed apartment buildings and shops. Donkey carts loaded with sugarcane trotted alongside the tracks headed for the markets in Luxor. A knock on the door behind my head startled me so badly I practically levitated off the floor.

"Luxor Station, madam."

Chapter Six

I STOOD IN THE Luxor Winter Palace Hotel's formal front garden and looked up at the twin curved staircases on either side of the entrance. The famous hotel had been our base of operations during the search for Hatshepsut in the Valley of the Kings across the Nile. I hadn't expected to be back only a few months later.

The hotel was built in 1907 by two Englishmen during the colonial period in Egypt, the same year Davis and Emma discovered KV55. Like a lot of historic buildings from that period, the hotel is an odd mixture of Edwardian and ancient Egyptian architecture. Corinthian columns across the front blossom at the tops into giant lotus flowers. Stained glass windows picture the Sphinx, the Great Pyramid, and Luxor Temple.

The revolving front door spun, and Cass and Alfi walked out. She shielded her eyes and gazed across the river toward the brown hills of the Valley of the Kings. She said something that made Alfi laugh and nod. They were dressed for fieldwork. Cass wore khaki pants, a shirt with the sleeves rolled up to her elbows, and calf-high brown leather boots. Alfi must have gotten Ministry of Antiquities approval for the expedition.

Cass's thick dark hair was tied back at the nape of her neck. She looked fantastic. Happy and comfortable in her skin. This is what life with her would be. She would never feel satisfied in a lecture hall at Columbia or Oxford or a laboratory in some museum. If I thought about it, as far as I knew she didn't even have a permanent home. For some reason, I felt shy about asking for details of her life outside archaeology.

She spotted me. She put her hands on her hips and stared. I took a deep breath and blew it out. Time to face the music. I climbed the stairs, bracing for Cass to be really angry that I disregarded her objections and came to Egypt, especially once I told her what happened on the train. I got halfway up and she came at me and grabbed me. I dropped my bag and clung to her. I wished I could hold on to the feeling of that moment forever. Her embrace told me she needed me. She wanted me with her. "Cass, you aren't angry?"

She glanced at Alfi and cleared her throat. Her strong reaction had embarrassed her. "I'm not angry. Knowing you, I think I would have been more surprised if you hadn't come. We'll deal with it. Leave your bag with the bellman. We need to get across the river and start work. The crew is waiting at KV55. You can take photos and keep the dig journal."

A dozen sailboats nodded and bobbed on their tethers in the small marina across from the hotel gardens. We boarded one, and I recognized the boatman. Cass read my mind again.

"Yes, it's Omar. I figured we owe him our loyalty for the scare he got the last time we were on the river in his boat. He watched the villainous Lord Dysart get eaten by the crocodile, as we did. The boat is by far the fastest way across the river toward the site. I've put Omar and his felucca on retainer for the duration of the dig."

"How long will that be?"

"It's hard to say before we see the state of the tomb. Davis resealed the entrance after his dig. That was sixty years ago. He thought he had emptied KV55 of all its antiquities. If, as I suspect, he missed the Queen's eye, he may have overlooked other treasures. We won't rush. I'm determined not to repeat Davis's rather slapdash approach."

We settled into the boat. The sail caught the wind, and Omar steered toward the strip of green across the river on the west bank. Cass dug in her bag and handed me a camera and a leatherbound journal.

Omar tied up at a wooden pier where Alfi's tiny white van waited in a palm tree's shade. We piled in the car and within half an hour stood before a padlocked iron door blocking the entrance to KV55. I shot a photo of the barrier. Two dozen workers gathered around Cass and Alfi as he snapped the old lock with giant bolt cutters and swung open the heavy metal door. The rusty hinges screeched in protest. Rubble completely blocked the entrance from the ground to within a foot of the ceiling. If Cass was disappointed about the obstruction, she didn't let on. I couldn't see her face but the set of her shoulders told me her determination to explore the tomb hadn't slacked.

Alfi didn't waste any time. He began organizing the workers to clear the entrance. A human relay line passed the rocks and sand in woven reed baskets hand to hand from the tomb to an examination area. This was what Cass meant about being careful. A bulldozer could have cleared the chamber in an hour, but precious artifacts might have been lost or destroyed.

Cass sat at a camp table under a canvas awning sifting the rubble. I took pictures and kept a running inventory of her finds. Right away she began turning up gold beads, tiny semiprecious stones that must have been pieces from a mosaic, and pottery shards. By the time the setting sun touched the mountains surrounding the valley, Alfi and the workers had uncovered twenty-one steps hewn from bedrock leading down to another sealed opening.

Cass yawned and stretched. "A good day. At this rate, even if we find more rubble in the antechamber, we'll have the way cleared to the burial chamber in four or five days." She took a folded paper from her pocket and smoothed it on the table in front of her. It was the Xerox page from Emma Andrews's diary showing her drawing of the wall painting of the boy presenting the chest to King Akhenaten. She tapped the paper. "That's where we'll find her eye."

I looked up from my notes and opened my mouth to ask what if the little chest in the painting held something other than Nefertiti's eye, when a glint of light from across the desert in the direction of the river caught my attention. The flash was the setting sun's reflection off some kind of lens like binoculars or a camera lens. Or a rifle scope!

Sometimes I act faster than I think. Witness when I dove into the crocodile-infested Nile after Hatshepsut's crystal got tossed in the water. This time I launched myself at Cass, knocking her to the ground, tipping over the camp table, and scattering rubble and relics.

Cass scrambled to her feet. "Bloody hell!"

I dropped behind the overturned table and pulled her down with me. "There's someone with a gun aimed at us."

"A gun? Where?"

I pointed toward the river.

She peeked over the edge of the table. "What did you see?"

"I'm not sure it's a gun, but..." A bullet striking the rock pile beside Cass interrupted me, showering us with sand and rubble shards. A second bullet whizzed over our heads. I held my breath and waited for the next shot.

Alfi skidded behind the table like he was sliding into third base. "He's firing from the ruins of the worker village. I saw the muzzle flash of the second shot. We can try and make it to the van."

Cass looked over her shoulder at the sun sinking behind the mountains. "It'll be dark soon. Let's wait a few minutes."

They sounded as calm as if they were discussing the next day's dig schedule. Meanwhile, my heart was beating out of my chest. "Cass, it must be the guy who was following us in Berlin. He was on the train from Cairo."

"You took a train from Cairo? Why didn't you fly?"

I rubbed the back of my neck in frustration. "That's not the important part right now. He must have been on the same plane I took from Berlin to Cairo and then followed me on the train from Cairo to Luxor. Another man, I think an Egyptian, pulled me out of my stateroom at gunpoint. He was trying to kidnap me or kill me or something. The Berlin guy showed up and jumped him. I think he threw him off the train. After that, the Berlin guy just disappeared again."

"Wait, slow down. You say the man from Berlin was on the Cairo to Luxor train?"

"Yes."

"That doesn't make any sense. Why would he follow you when you were supposed to go to New York? Why didn't he follow me to Luxor?"

I shrugged. "Maybe there were two of them at the Berlin airport. One to follow you and another for me. Anyway, the shoe guy's here in Luxor, and that's probably him shooting at us."

Cass tapped her finger against her lips. "Why would he save you on the train and then try to shoot you? Did he say anything during the encounter?"

I replayed the scene in my mind. "Not a peep."

In the fading light Alfi scanned the jagged line of the ruined wall that in antiquity had enclosed the worker village. "No sign of the shooter. The daylight's gone." He stood and dusted off his pants. "I'll give the workers their orders to come back tomorrow?"

Cass nodded. "Will they stick with us?"

"Most will. We may lose a few." He started toward the tomb. "I'll bring the van closer for you. I'll sleep out here tonight."

"Are you concerned for your safety?"

Instead of answering, Alfi opened his khaki vest to show a chrome revolver stuck in his waistband. He trotted off to get the van.

Cass pushed her sleeves above her elbows. I helped her right the table. She switched on a flashlight, and we began retrieving the scattered relics.

I gathered a handful of gold beads that lay scattered in the sand. "I suppose we have to call the police. I'm not looking forward to seeing Inspector Saleem again." I pictured the rumpled police detective who investigated Cass and me for murder a few months before.

She picked up the copy of the page from Emma Andrews's diary, folded it, and put it back in her pocket. "Calling the police is the last thing I want to do. Saleem will shut down the dig. Only a few days and some rubble separate us from the burial chamber." She straightened with her hands on her hips and gazed toward the river. "The shooter was trying to scare us."

In my case, that tactic worked.

Chapter Seven

CASS AND I FACED each other in the boat's stern with our knees touching. The air and water were eerily still. Without wind for the sail, Omar would have to row us back across the river. He furled the mainsail, fitted two long oars into oarlocks, and shoved away from shore. The sky and river blended in inky blackness. The only illumination was from an olive oil lamp hanging on a hook on the mast. The lamp looked ancient enough to have been discovered in one of the Valley of the Kings tombs. I leaned to Cass and whispered, "How can he see where we're going with just the light from that lamp?"

"The light is for our benefit. Omar can make this crossing blindfolded."

I let my hand trail over the side of the boat in the water and rested my forehead on my arm. "Do you think I brought the danger with me? The guy followed me from Berlin."

"They would have come with or without you."

That made me feel a little better.

The lamp swung back and forth in time with Omar's oar strokes. I closed my eyes, and the next thing I knew the bow of the boat bumped against the marina pier in front of the hotel. I wiped my mouth. "I fell asleep. Did I snore?"

"Not that I heard." Cass stood and held the boat against the dock while Omar tied us up. "Some food and a good night's sleep will do us both good. Let's get you checked in and we'll order dinner in our room."

Inside the elegant reception hall of the Winter Palace I half expected to see Berlin guy lounging in one of the leather chairs in front of the fire, but the room was deserted except for two hotel employees on ladders taking down strings of lights from a thirty-foot Christmas tree. I checked in at reception and recovered my suitcase from the bellman, and we took the elevator to our suite on the top floor. Cass picked up the phone. "What do you want for dinner?"

"You decide."

She blew out a breath. "Something quick and simple." She ordered sandwiches and wine. "I'm worn out and I can only imagine how tired you are. When did you last sleep?"

I had to think a minute. "The night before we left Berlin. Seems like a month ago. I didn't get any rest on the train." I shook my head to clear the memory of the gun barrel in my back.

"Good thing you're young." She went into the bathroom. I leaned against the doorjamb and watched her strip off her khaki shirt without unbuttoning it and drop it on the floor. She turned on the water and bent over the basin, scrubbing her face with her hands. Her naked breasts hung silhouetted against the tile shower wall. I moved behind her, took them in my hands, and massaged the firm flesh. The nipples hardened in my palms. "I thought about you on the train."

"Do you mean the train you took from Cairo to Luxor when you were supposed to be on a plane to New York?"

"Yes, that one." I encircled her waist with one arm and pulled her into me. "Don't you want to know what I was thinking?" She stopped scrubbing and smiled at our reflections in the mirror. She pressed into me.

I whispered in her ear. "I was thinking about your breasts and the first time we made love in this very hotel. Do you remember?" She gave the familiar, sexy chuckle from her diaphragm, then turned and took my face in her hands and kissed me.

The knock from room service interrupted. "Damn." I held up a finger. "You wait here. I'll get it."

Even for our modest order, the dinner service was formal. All snowy linen tablecloth and napkins, sterling silver, crystal, and bone china. I heard water running in Cass's bath. I shifted from foot to foot while the waiter went through a whole wine ritual.

First, he presented the wine bottle for my inspection like it was his prized possession. Then he pulled the cork with a pop and handed it to me, waiting expectantly for a response. I nodded because I was not sure what else to do. He seemed satisfied and poured an inch of wine.

In the bathroom, the water stopped. I pictured nude Cass stepping into the tub. I was anxious to finish the wine ceremony and pick up where she and I left off. I drained the glass. "Good." I signed the check with a big tip and practically shoved him out the door.

I juggled the wine bottle and glasses and opened the bathroom door. Cass was up to her chin in bubbles. Tendrils of steam rising from the water filled the bathroom with an exotic scent.

"Can I come in with you?"

She smiled and nodded.

I set the wine and glasses on the floor beside the tub, stripped off my boots and clothes, and climbed in facing her with my legs wrapped around her waist. "What is that fragrance?"

She held a bar of soap under my nose. "Susinum. It's made with lily, myrrh, and cinnamon. It's an ancient scent. Nefertiti herself no doubt used the perfume in her bath."

She worked up a lather and began massaging my shoulders and neck.

"That feels wonderful. Don't stop." I closed my eyes and sank lower in the water. "Cass, why does a waiter want you to inspect the cork he pops out of a wine bottle? What are you supposed to look for?"

"It's mostly ceremony, but there's a practical reason too. If the cork is wet or smells musty, the wine may have gone bad."

She moved to rubbing my breasts. "Is this okay?"

"Mm. Nice. What about the little taste of wine they give you?"

"It's not about the taste. It's more the smell. You swirl the glass, and if the wine smells of a wet dog or an old attic, you send the bottle back." She made more suds and rubbed along my spine down to my buttocks.

"Have you ever sent wine back?"

"Rarely. Only once or twice." She began kneading my buttocks.

At that point I forgot all about the wine and sank into her touch. Her slick fingers found and slowly traced the cleft between my buttocks from the back to the front over and over. She went inside me. "Do you like this?" Her voice was a throaty whisper.

I tried to say yes, but the sound came out a whimper. I got that feeling you get just before you climax that you wish would last forever, but if the sensation did last forever you'd probably die from it. Then I came, and she pulled me into her arms so fast and strong we both slid underwater and came up sputtering and laughing. "Let's eat our dinner before I drown you."

We dried each other with thick towels with big gold *WPs* monogrammed on them.

I picked up the bottle. "What about the wine?"

"Bring it. We'll eat our supper in bed."

Chapter Eight

THE NEXT MORNING, AFTER we crossed the river in Omar's sailboat, Cass and I loaded our gear in the van and headed for KV55. Cass drove while I checked my notes from the day before. The journal left off mid-sentence at the moment I saw the flash of the rifle scope and knocked the table over.

"I hope Alfi had a quiet night and the sniper didn't come back."

Cass nodded. "I trust him to take care of himself."

That's exactly what I said back in our Berlin hotel room when I was trying to make a case for coming to Egypt—that I could take care of myself. That plan didn't work out so well. "I still think we ought to call the police. The bad guys may not remain satisfied with scaring us."

"Let's see how the work progresses today."

At the tomb, Alfi waited with the bolt cutters to open the antechamber entry at the base of the steps. I held my breath as he swung open the iron door. Would the space be full of rubble? Cass swept her flashlight around the plastered walls. "This is very good. The best news." Rocks and debris a foot or so deep covered the floors, but compared with the stairway the antechamber was almost clear. At first the ceiling and walls appeared decorated, but when my eyes adjusted to the gloom I saw that what I took for wall paintings on the plaster surfaces were water stains. The sloping floor of the long, narrow room led west to an opening in the back wall.

Cass stepped to the south wall and motioned me over. "Take some close shots of the water damage."

I pointed to the opening. "Isn't that the burial chamber? With Emma's wall painting? Aren't we going to look for the eye?"

"First things first. We'll clear this area before we proceed."

I shrugged. "And you accuse me of being linear?"

"We don't want to repeat Davis's mistakes by being careless."

"Can't we just take a peek?"

Cass shined the light into the burial chamber. The room was smaller than I had expected. It was only about ten feet square and looked empty aside from plaster that had fallen from the walls and ceiling and a granite sarcophagus in the middle. The gray stone crypt looked more like a horse trough than the final resting place of a king. The wall painting in the corner Emma had copied in her journal offered the only color in the room.

Cass and I went outside and took up our positions under the canvas awning. The workers formed their relay line and began a hypnotic singsong chant, part spoken and part sung. Half of them recited a few words. The other half responded with a different phrase, then they repeated the whole thing.

"What are they saying?"

"They're praising Amun, the god of gods, then complimenting Alfi for being a good boss."

The workers' reed baskets produced more pottery shards, gold beads, and semi precious stones similar to the ones we found the day before, but also some new stuff like gold-leafed pieces of wood and glass lotus leaves and poppy petals that Cass said were probably parts of an ornate collar like the one on Nefertiti's bust.

I couldn't help glancing every few minutes across the desert to the ruined wall around the worker village. There were no signs of the sniper having returned.

By noon Alfi reported the antechamber had been cleared. Cass pushed away from the camp table. "Time to examine the burial chamber." Her voice was even but her hand trembled as she picked up the flashlight. I checked the camera for film and grabbed my journal. I followed her down the stone steps and across the sloping antechamber floor. She paused at the burial chamber opening.

"Cass." She turned and I snapped her picture. After all these years it's still my favorite photo of her. The image captures what I saw outside the Winter Palace Hotel. She was exactly who and where she should be, the determined scientist discovering echoes of our shared human past. In the picture her expression is a mix of excited anticipation and an odd sadness. When I took the shot, I made a note in my journal to ask her later about the reason for her sorrow.

She followed her flashlight beam into the room, and Alfi and I went in after her. In the corner, there it was—the only adornment in the whole tomb as far as I could tell. Cass's flashlight illuminated the wall painting Emma Andrews copied into her diary over sixty years before. Emma had done a pretty good job, but seeing the three thousand year old original version was something else. Over King Akhenaten's mummy and the kneeling boy, Aten the sun god emitted rays of light. One ray pointed straight down toward the floor and ended in a drawing of a left eye lined in kohl. It might as well have said, "Dig Here For Nefertiti's Eye."

Alfi brought the workers in to remove the paving stone directly under the eye. The paver was not cemented in place but fitted snugly against adjacent ones. The workers used a crowbar to get a fingerhold, then two men lifted it. They looked at Cass for orders. She motioned them away and began digging with a trowel. About a foot down, she stopped. "There's something." She switched to a paintbrush and swept sand from the tip of an object that looked like a rolled-up piece of old cloth. "It's a papyrus."

"Sayid Alfi!" The shout came from the top of the steps.

Alfi led the way above ground. A worker pointed toward the battered yellow Renault with a blue light on the roof parked at the edge of our site. Detective Inspector Saleem of the Luxor Police leaned against the hood with his arms folded. I couldn't help letting out a little groan. Someone must have called the police about yesterday's gunshots. Just when we were getting close to our goal, Cass's fear that Saleem could shut down the dig might be coming true.

The detective wore a gray suit and wrinkled white shirt with a tie that looked like he knotted it in the dark. A narrow-brimmed fedora hat showed a scruffy fringe of dark hair around the brim. He pushed away from the car and ambled over to our group with his hands in his pockets. "Dr. Stillwell, welcome back to Luxor." He peered around her at the tomb opening and stated the obvious. "Digging again."

"We are, Detective Inspector, and we're quite busy at the moment. What can I do for you today?"

"Certainly." He took a small spiral notebook and pencil from his jacket pocket and deliberately flipped pages. "Let us get to the point." He cleared his throat and licked the pencil lead. "It appears the Governorate has received a call regarding..." He read from the notebook. "An unauthorized disturbance in the Valley of the Kings in the vicinity of Tutankhamun's royal tomb." He gestured to the west. "Which I believe lies a few hundred yards away from where we stand."

Cass tucked a stray lock of hair behind her ear. "A call from whom about what sort of disturbance?"

He took off his hat and scratched his head with the eraser end of his pencil. "That is part of the difficulty. The caller was anonymous and his description of the nature of the disturbance vague. As you can imagine, we felt reluctant to credit the call. Much the same as you, we are very busy. But the referral is from the Governorate's office after all, so..." He shrugged and smiled. "We can clear this up quickly, no doubt. May I see your Ministry of Antiquities authorization for excavation at this site?"

"If you need to see the written approval, the papers are safely at the Winter Palace."

He turned his palms up and shrugged. "Were the decision up to me I would take you at your word. But you understand...the Governorate's office..."

Cass blew out a frustrated breath. "Can we meet at the hotel this evening? Say, six o'clock. I'll be happy to produce the authorization."

"Just so. Six at the Winter Palace."

Cass turned on her heel and started toward the tomb opening with Alfi following.

"And Dr. Stillwell..." Saleem pointed his pencil toward the tomb. "Until this matter is cleared up, I must ask that you and your workmen refrain from entering KV55." He doffed his hat with a little bow and headed for the Renault. We watched him drive away.

Cass said something under her breath and started back toward the tomb entrance.

I ran after her and drew her aside away from the workmen. "Cass, no matter how dumb this is, you can't go back inside yet. You're on the verge of an amazing discovery, and there's no reason to get in a conflict with the government over the permit. We'll show it to Saleem tonight and get back in the tomb first thing tomorrow."

"It's a ridiculous waste of time."

"I know, but we may need Saleem's help. Somebody or several somebodies are trying to sabotage our finding the eye. They're even willing to shoot at us. They're the ones who called the police. What about that?"

She walked a few steps toward the tomb entrance then turned back. She shook her head. "You're right."

I felt a little lightheaded with relief.

Cass called to Alfi. "Can you and the workers sleep here overnight to guard the tomb and for an early start in the morning? Ari and I will crate up our finds so far."

Cass and I began packing the forgotten remnants of Davis's 1907 dig in cotton-lined crates for shipping to the Cairo Museum. I checked off each item to verify my inventory.

She nestled a handful of mosaic glass pieces in the packing. "These leftovers are the result of Davis's slapdash approach. He was more interested in discovering tombs than excavating them and protecting the contents. Let's finish up and get back across the river."

Chapter Nine

WE STEPPED OFF THE elevator as the massive grandfather clock beside the registration desk chimed six. Cass looked around the lobby. "He's not here yet. Let's have a cocktail." The evening manager, Samut Paneb, rushed over to seat us at a quiet table in the lounge. "Thank you, Sam. This will do nicely."

The young man bowed deeply. "My pleasure, Dr. Stillwell. I'm glad to have an opportunity to say how happy I am to have you and Miss Morgan back." He looked from Cass to me and back to Cass. "What may I serve you?"

Cass put the manila folder with her dig approval documents on the table between us. "I'll have a Manhattan straight up very chilled. Ari?"

"I'll have the same." I was trying to develop a taste for the strong cocktail. I thought the name sounded sophisticated. A Manhattan looks tasty—rich mahogany brown and garnished with a bright red cherry. I'm pretty sure no one in Beaufort, North Carolina knows how to make one.

Sam bowed again. "Right away."

Cass opened the folder and straightened the papers. "Our reunion with Detective Inspector Saleem should be simple and brief."

I hoped she was right. I pictured Cass and me relaxing on our suite balcony sipping a second Manhattan, the breeze from the river ruffling the soft curls around her face.

She squirmed in her chair. "He'll see our approval is in order. We need to get back in the tomb to unearth the papyrus and find the eye."

You could tell Cass didn't have much patience with Saleem. She's so smart that she sometimes struggles to hide her judgment of people who aren't as quick as she is. She's a lot like Gran that way. One of my grandmother's favorite expressions is "He's not the sharpest tool in the shed, bless his heart." The *bless his heart* part is the Southern way to say something negative about someone and still be nice.

But Gran also says, "Don't cut off your nose to spite your face." She means don't be your own worst enemy. We helped Saleem solve a murder only a few months ago. There might be an opportunity to ask him to return the favor. We might enlist his help with finding whoever was trying to derail our search for the Queen's eye. "When are you going to tell him we got shot at?"

"I'm not sure yet whom we can trust." She looked past me. "Here he is now."

Saleem stood in the archway in his same rumpled suit minus the fedora. He spotted us and strolled over. "Dr. Stillwell. Miss Morgan." He pulled out a chair and sat. "My apologies for this inconvenience. You have many important calls on your time, I'm sure. But you understand a referral from the Governorate…"

He had the annoying habit of never finishing a sentence once the Governorate came up.

Cass passed the manila folder across the table to Saleem. "This should answer the question. You'll notice the signature of the Minister himself on our approval."

Saleem took reading glasses from his jacket pocket, licked his fingers, and thumbed through the papers. "Ah, your application states you are 'applying modern archaeological techniques to a 1907 expedition that may have missed important findings.' And that you plan 'to benefit the Egyptian people.' Commendable, commendable." He took off his glasses. "What important findings do you expect to discover?"

Sam interrupted with our drinks. "Detective Inspector, may I serve you?"

"Just tea, Mr. Paneb." He smiled at us. "On duty, you know." Saleem hitched up his pants and leaned back in his chair. He was getting too comfortable for Cass's hope the meeting would be simple and brief.

He leaned forward and looked around the room. "Do you have a theory about what your expedition might discover? Mind you, those details are the purview of the Ministry of Antiquities. My curiosity is merely as an interested amateur and someone proud of my people's history."

Cass sipped her drink. "As with your investigations, Detective Inspector, we must remain open-minded."

"Ah yes. And at the same time we collect clues like puzzle pieces that fill in a picture we may have suspected all along."

Cass could have pointed out how off the mark Saleem's puzzle picture was when we were here searching for Hatshepsut. He suspected us of murder and ultimately arrested the wrong man. It was only with Cass's help that the real murderer was brought to justice. She restrained herself from mentioning his miscalculations.

Sam rushed up. "Detective Inspector, a phone call for you. They say it's an emergency."

I watched the policeman follow Sam across the lobby. I took too big a drink of my Manhattan and suppressed a cough. "If he's being truthful about his pride in Egypt's heritage and if it turns out we can trust him, he might become an ally, right?"

Sam approached the table. "Dr. Stillwell, the call for Detective Inspector Saleem. There's been a shooting at KV55! Saleem has left."

"Alfi may be in trouble." Cass grabbed the manila folder. "Put this in the safe, Sam." We ran to the front door and watched the yellow Renault speed away to the south with blue lights flashing. "He's likely to shut down KV55 for good. He's headed for the bridge across the river at Ponti di Luxor. If we hurry and the wind cooperates, we can beat him to the dig by half an hour or more."

We found Omar smoking and chatting with the other boatmen at the marina. A stiff breeze helped us make record time across the river to the white van. Cass floor-boarded it to the dig. We skidded to a stop beside a cluster of workers with Alfi in the middle holding a bloody cloth against a worker's shoulder. Cass made her way into the circle. "Alfi, is he all right?"

"The bullet grazed his arm. There were two gunmen. They drove away in a black Range Rover."

"White men?"

"No, two Egyptians. Their purpose seemed to be to scare away the workers."

"Alfi, see to the wounded man. Ari, you come with me. We must uncover the papyrus. We have only a few minutes before Saleem gets here."

Cass handed me a paintbrush, and we cleared away sand around the papyrus. She tenderly lifted an ancient scroll and unfurled it on the burial chamber floor. "Oh…" Her voice trailed off. She covered her face and took a deep breath. When she looked up, there were tears in her eyes. "It's the sculptor's blueprint for the Nefertiti bust. Thutmose drew this diagram to aid him in getting the proportions right."

I leaned over her shoulder. "She has both eyes."

A commotion on the stairs at the tomb entrance interrupted. Saleem muttered a few words that sounded like "Damn it!" except in Arabic and stumbled into the burial chamber. "Dr. Stillwell, I must insist you and your men clear the area while I sort out this matter."

Cass carefully rolled the papyrus. "You can't shut us down, Detective Inspector. You saw the Minister's permission papers. We're on the verge of an important discovery. Our dig must go forward. You said yourself you have no authority over the expedition."

"No, but a shooting is my responsibility. I must apprehend the attackers and assure your safety in the meantime."

The two stared at each other at an impasse. The time had come to avoid cutting off our noses to spite our faces. The Queen's eye might be a few feet away. Trust or no trust, we needed Saleem's cooperation. I stepped between them. "Maybe you can find a way to accomplish both. Cass, it's time to tell him."

She told Saleem part of the story, the part where we were looking for Nefertiti's missing eye and some people—she said we didn't know who exactly, which was true—were trying to stop us. She didn't go into why they might be interested in stopping us. We didn't know that for sure either. Her account was enough to convince the detective to give us twenty-four hours to search for the eye in KV55. He set up shop under the awning outside the tomb and began interviewing witnesses to the shooting, and Alfi and the workers started digging in the burial chamber.

They labored all night and half the next day, removing each paver stone and digging down to bedrock.

Cass stood with her hands on her hips in the middle of a dozen five-foot-high sand piles. "It's not here." She said the words like she couldn't believe she hadn't found the eye, but that she had to accept it. She blew a wisp of hair out of her eyes. "I need a cigarette."

Her smoking worries me sometimes, but she does it only when she's particularly disturbed or upset. I followed her up the steps to Alfi's van. She dug in her bag. "I didn't bring my cigarettes. Bloody hell!"

She plopped down in the passenger seat. "The eye was in the tomb. The wall painting says so, and someone hid the papyrus there alongside it."

"Why would someone take the eye and leave the papyrus?"

"It may have been a worker who missed the blueprint's importance. We've always known workers stole pieces from Davis's KV55 dig. Gold straps from the coffin and a vulture necklace from the mummy showed up on the black market in 1907. Rumors are that Davis himself often traded in antiquities. He used a dealer named Mohammed Dharam in Cairo."

She placed the papyrus in her bag and stood up, then called Alfi over. "When Saleem finishes, we'll stow these crates in the tomb and lock the entrance. Get a few hours' rest and meet us in the hotel lobby at first light tomorrow. We're driving to Cairo. My bet is the eye passed through Mohammed Dharam's hands."

Chapter Ten

AFTER DINNER IN THE hotel dining room, we went into the lounge. Cass wanted a brandy. A few other hotel guests chatted quietly in groups of twos and threes. We passed an attractive youngish woman sitting alone reading a book, *Egyptian Gods from Anubis to Zenenet.* Clever. We found a table in the corner. Cass sipped her brandy while I leaned on my elbows and fought dozing off.

"Excuse me. Dr. Stillwell?" It was the young woman with the book. "I hope I'm not disturbing you." She stuck out her hand. "Olympia Shaunessy. I'm a huge fan. I followed your search for Hatshepsut from your first articles in the journals to the news of her discovery."

This fan probably read the snarky editorial replies to Cass's early journal articles when the establishment was dismissing her theories about Hatshepsut as pages out of a pulp fiction novel.

"Olympia Shaunessy?"

"Yes, I know it's a mouthful. My mother was from Crete and my father was from Dublin. Call me Pia." She glanced at the empty chair.

Cass nodded at me. "This is my assistant, Ari Morgan."

I wished she'd use some title other than assistant, but what would it be? Colleague? Partner? Girlfriend?

Pia offered her hand to me. She cleared her throat and looked at the empty seat again.

Cass pulled out the chair. "Join us." She nodded at Pia's book. "You're interested in Egyptian gods?"

"Oh, I'm sort of an amateur armchair archeologist. I hesitate to even say that to you. Mostly I study other people's work I read about in books. I suspect trained archaeologists have nothing but disdain for amateurs."

"Many do, but where would we be without untrained amateurs such as Lord Carnarvon and Theodore Davis? I've observed that breakthroughs have more to do with passion, luck, and persistence than training. Training does improve dig techniques, but they are better learned on-site than in a classroom."

Pia relaxed into her chair a little and marked her place in her book. "My passion lies in research. Digging through obscure writings in the stacks of New York City Public Library and the archives of MOMA. This is my first ever in-person visit to a real site. I've splurged on this trip to Luxor to study firsthand the wall paintings in Senenmut's tomb where you found Hatshepsut."

Cass patted my hand. "Yes, we found her. Hatshepsut's beloved counselor Senenmut hid her in his own unfinished tomb. He saved her mummy from the wrath of her stepson, but I suspect you're interested in something different in Senenmut's tomb, the painting of the Minoan tribute processional."

"Yes, how did you know the painting is my interest?"

"You mentioned your connection with Crete. The tomb painting is the oldest evidence we have so far of a trade connection between ancient Greece and Egypt."

Pia clapped her hands. Her green eyes teared up with emotion. "Yes. Seeing the procession of Cretan warriors in honor of Hatshepsut was such a thrill. I sensed the connection between my roots and this ancient place that no picture in a book could have provided."

I felt like a fifth wheel. One of Gran's sayings came to mind. "Worthless as chewing gum on a boot heel." Cass and Pia were having a connection that left me sitting on the sidelines.

Cass sipped her brandy. "Your passion is archaeology. What do you work at full time?"

"I suppose you could call my full-time job my passion too. I teach Advanced Placement calculus at public high school in the Bronx."

I cleared my throat and jumped in the conversation. "Pia, I'll admit I don't even know what the word calculus means."

They both looked at me and blinked. Pia nodded. "Most people don't. Everyone's familiar with algebra and geometry."

I conjured a picture of Mrs. Dixon, my Algebra II teacher in high school. I doubted she'd describe me as familiar with algebra.

Pia went on. "Geometry and algebra measure values at a particular point in time. They're static, but in the real world things are constantly changing. Calculus is a branch of mathematics that measures change. How variations in one set of factors affect others over time."

The expression on my face must have given away how clueless I felt. I regretted letting my insecurity push me into the middle of their conversation. I was embarrassing myself.

Pia went on in the patient voice I suspected she used as a teacher. "In practical terms, calculus can measure how inflation affects the cost of a gallon of milk or how gravitational pull among the planets impacts satellite orbits."

Thank goodness at that point Cass bailed me out. She drank the last of her brandy. "Shall we, Ari? We have an early morning. It was nice meeting you, Pia."

Pia jumped up so fast she had to catch her chair to keep it upright. "I hope I'm not being presumptuous, but if I can ever help you, I would be honored." She wrote a New York phone number on a cocktail napkin and handed it to Cass. She looked from Cass to me. She said again, "I hope I haven't interrupted."

Cass put her arm around my waist and started toward the elevator. "Good luck with your exploration of the tomb painting."

"I'm flying home to New York tomorrow, but the trip and seeing the tomb in person have been the experience of a lifetime. And meeting you is the icing on the cake."

On the elevator ride Cass kept her arm around me. "She's an intelligent and interesting young woman."

"And attractive too." I studied Cass's face for a reaction and struggled to keep the green-eyed monster in check. Like I told Eleanor Frame at that coffee kiosk, I crave reassurance of Cass's feelings for me.

"Yes, gorgeous red hair." She kissed me on the cheek.

* * * * *

The next morning at dawn we started for Cairo in Alfi's little van to discover if the antiquities dealer Mohammed Dharam might have had some connection with Nefertiti's eye. Across the river, the west bank was still dark. Beyond the tree line, balloons lifted tourists over the Valley of the Kings. The fires heating the air under the balloons' colorful canopies burned bright orange against the brown hills. The excursions set out at dawn to avoid the turbulence of warm air later in the day. Cass sat in the van's front seat beside Alfi, and I shared the back seat with gas cans filled with extra fuel for the eight-hour drive.

Cass and Alfi kept up a low-level buzz of conversation in the front seat. The van didn't have air conditioning, so all the windows were down. The heavy desert wind buffeted my eardrums and made it impossible to make out their words. I snuggled into the corner of the seat and watched a flock of migrating birds lift off the river's surface. They were headed south to the enormous man-made lake at the new Aswan dam. They rose in unison like a giant billowing white blanket. Have you ever wondered how they elect the head bird to signal the exact time to move on?

We had the highway to ourselves except for a few donkey carts piled high with sugarcane and an occasional rattletrap truck hauling camels to market. I felt sorry for the majestic animals packed nose to tail in the tight space. The road was straight as an arrow as far as the eye could see. I thought about something Gran said once describing the drive across the Panhandle of Texas. "It's so flat you can watch your dog run away from home for a week." I pictured Gran and Mom and their cozy cottage in Beaufort, North

Carolina and remembered the first time I went home after starting college in New York. I opened the front door and a familiar smell enveloped me that said, "Here's where you're loved."

I drifted off to sleep feeling homesick. After some time, no idea how long, I jerked awake. The smell wasn't of my North Carolina home, but of gasoline sloshing around in the canisters beside me in the back seat. Something about the road or the car had changed. The little van was moving a lot faster. Cass and Alfi had stopped chatting. Cass was turned all the way around in her seat staring out the back window. Alfi kept glancing in the rearview mirror. A car lagged behind us keeping a steady pace. A black Range Rover. The kind the two men who shot up our dig site drove.

Alfi took his gun out of his waistband and handed it to Cass.

Cass checked the revolver for bullets. "There are two men. I can see the passenger has a rifle. We'll be outgunned."

"We can't outrun them. I'm going to slow down and see what they do." He slowed to half speed. The Range Rover backed off to maintain four or five car lengths. Alfi speeded up and they matched us. "Ari, take the cap off one of the gas cans and hand it up front. There's a road flare under the seat. Do you see it?"

I passed the gas can to Cass and found the flare.

Alfi glanced in the rearview mirror again. "Do you know how to light it? Take the white cap off the end. When the time comes, I'll give the word. Use the cap to strike the flare like a match." He pointed down the road. "We're coming up on a camel truck. Once we get just past it, things will happen fast, so hold on."

Alfi stomped on the accelerator. The little van shuttered and lurched ahead. The passenger in the Range Rover stuck his rifle out the side window and fired a shot. Alfi swerved across the center line. We whizzed around the camel truck and Alfi cut the wheel hard to the right. We flew off the highway. The van tipped on two wheels and balanced for a heart-stopping instant before bouncing back on all fours and coming to rest up to its axle in sand.

The camel truck driver hit his brakes and skidded across the road to a stop on the opposite shoulder, causing the gangly animals to fall into each other in a tangle of legs. The whole mass of them started braying their protest. The Range Rover pulled off the road and two guys with rifles jumped out. Cass, Alfi, and I ducked behind the van.

"Light the flare!" I struck the flare like Alfi told me and thank goodness it caught the first time. He flung the open gas can like an Olympic shot-putter toward the Range Rover. It landed on the roof. Alfi counted to five and took the burning flare from me and tossed it next to the gas can. The Range Rover exploded in flames. The gunmen stumbled across the road to the camel truck and pulled the driver from the cab. They U-turned and took off toward Luxor with the camels still bellowing and trying to scramble to their feet.

Cass went to help the truck driver, and Alfi opened the tailgate of the van and pulled out two shovels. He handed me one, and we began clearing sand away from the back wheels.

"How did you know that gas can trick would work?"

Alfi wiped his brow with his sleeve and grinned. "I saw it once in an American movie."

We gave the truck driver a ride to the next village. He spouted a running monologue in Arabic that sounded like curses against the men who took his camels. He kept saying "Almafya, Almafya."

"What is he saying?"

"He recognized the men as part of a gang that steals and traffics black-market antiquities. He is entreating the Gods to send their wrath down on the crooks."

Cass lit a cigarette, shielding the flame from wind blowing in her window. "He calls them the Egyptian Mafia."

"Is that who has been after us all along? The guy on the train, the sniper at the dig, and these two?"

"Most likely. There's a lot of incentive. Illegal trading in antiquities is a huge business, perhaps billions each year. Modern Egypt is built on top of ancient Egypt, so people can dig in their own courtyards and discover treasures. Organized gangs swoop in and loot dig sites both big and small, and they raid museums even in broad daylight. It's impossible to guard all the treasures. The booty is passed on to the international black market through the country's ports and porous borders."

"Why doesn't the government do something about it?"

The truck driver interrupted. "Almafya!"

"Some people accuse the authorities of having a hand in the process, even the police and military."

"Yeah. I remember Lord Dysart bribed the Minister of Antiquities for a dig permit the last time we were in Luxor. You don't think Detective Inspector Saleem is in on it, do you?"

"Hard to know."

"So we're in the middle between Hitler Youth who want to restore Nefertiti's eye and thereby the glory of the Third Reich, and the Egyptian Mafia who want to sell the eye to the highest bidder."

Cass blew out smoke and nodded. "Nefertiti's eye would mean a huge payday for the gang. Millions. And restoring the bust would shower enormous attention and prestige on the country that possesses her."

Maybe the truck driver was right. Maybe we needed the wrath of the Gods for reinforcements.

Chapter Eleven

THE ANTIQUITIES SHOP WAS in the heart of Cairo, in a section called Al Musky, one of the city's most important marketplaces. Alfi steered the van around cars, pedestrians, and donkey carts. Cass had insisted I sit up front with Alfi for the last leg of our journey. She was doubled up in the back, her knees under her chin. Women in scarves fingered fruits and vegetables on the sidewalks outside the shops and men gathered in twos and threes discussing who knows what big issues of the day at the tops of their lungs. We came to an alley entrance too narrow even for Alfi's small van, and he parked at the curb.

I helped Cass out of the cramped back seat. The smell in the air was what you noticed first. Some kind of herb or incense aroma floated over the crowd. The scent was not exactly unpleasant, just unfamiliar. Alfi led us halfway down the alley to a storefront painted oxblood red. Over the door, fancy gold script announced *Dharam Bros. Antiquities* in English and then some Arabic after that. The front window displayed pottery, stone figurines, and ornate bangles and necklaces.

I pressed close to the window. "Are those real?"

Cass nodded. "The Dharam brothers have been selling antiquities for four generations. They might deal in black-market artifacts from time to time, but I doubt they would risk their reputations with fakes."

Alfi pushed the shop door open and stood back to let us go in first. A little brass bell tinkled, but the sound died at the doorway, baffled by heavy velvet drapes covering the ceiling and walls. They gave the shop the feel of being inside a Bedouin tent. Cass led the way into the room. The smell of incense from the street seemed to concentrate in the showroom where every table and glass display case was crammed with antiquities.

"Hello?" Cass stopped and waited. No answer. I figured the shop owner didn't hear the bell when we came in. There were two doors in the back wall, both standing open. One led outside to the alley and the other into an office. Cass gestured to Alfi, and he walked to the back of the shop and stuck his head inside the office door. "Sayid Dharam?" Alfi disappeared inside. "Dr. Stillwell, come quickly!"

The room was tiny and windowless with barely enough space for a desk and the antique black safe with the door standing open. Account books littered the desktop and covered the floor as though someone had riffled through them searching for something. An old-fashioned black telephone on the desk lay turned on its side with the receiver off the hook.

Behind the desk, a dark-bearded middle-aged man stared unseeing past us into the showroom. He wore Western clothes, an expensive-looking navy blue suit and starched white shirt. A red stain bloomed in the middle of his chest around the hilt of a gold dagger. Alfi went behind the desk and felt for the pulse in his neck. He shook his head. "Dead."

Cass, Alfi, and I stared at the dead man. We had just missed the killer. The red stain around the dagger's hilt in the middle of his chest was still spreading on his white shirt.

Cass looked inside the antique black safe's open door. "Nothing." She began picking up and discarding account books. "Alfi, lock the front and back doors. Ari, help me find any logs dated around 1907. We may have interrupted the killer before he found what he was looking for."

I tried to ignore the dead body and concentrated on spotting the oldest-looking books. I found 1907 on the bottom of a pile dating back to the turn of the century. Cass began scanning the pages of purchases and sales by date. She found an entry. "Here's something on April 12, 1907, four months after Davis discovered the opening to the tomb. The entry says Mohammed Dharam purchased sundry articles from KV55 for seventy-five pounds sterling."

"That doesn't sound like very much money."

"About a hundred dollars US back then. Today that's three thousand. For a tomb worker, that's a fortune. Now if we can find the sale from Dharam to a third party." She ran her finger down the column. "Here's an entry. Just two weeks later on April 28. 'Sold to Mr. Theodore M. Davis for one hundred fifty pounds sterling.' Davis bought back the articles that someone had stolen from the tomb he excavated."

"Ahron!" The anguished cry came from the office doorway behind us. A stooped elderly man grabbed for the edge of the wall. His legs gave way and he slumped to the floor. He buried his head in his hands and moaned something in Arabic. Alfi rushed to his side and lifted him up. He guided him outside the tiny office into a chair in the showroom and exchanged a few words. "He is Shakir Dharam. He asks why have we murdered his brother. I explained that we found him like this, and the same people who harmed Ahron are targeting us."

The man moaned again and said in English, "What did they want?" He looked around the shop. "They could have taken anything and spared his life."

Cass knelt beside him. "Mr. Dharam, they were looking for information about a relic from KV55 that may have passed through your shop in 1907. A small rosewood chest holding the missing eye from Nefertiti's bust."

Dharam shook his head. "That cursed eye has plagued my family for generations."

"So you've seen it?" Cass glanced at me. "Please tell us."

"I was only a boy when my jaadi, my grandfather, first acquired the eye, and Ahron was not yet even born." He glanced toward the office and tried to get up from the chair. "I must call his wife."

Cass put her hand on his arm. "Mr. Dharam, anything you can tell us may help bring these people to justice."

He fell back in the chair. "My grandfather bought it along with other relics from tomb workers. Jaadi suspected the pieces came from a dig in the Valley of the Kings funded by Theodore Davis, who was a long-standing client. He contacted Mr. Davis and sold the artifacts—including the eye in the chest inscribed with Thutmose's name—back to him for a modest profit. The sale to Mr. Davis would have been the end of our story with the Queen's eye except that a few years later the German found her bust missing the left eye in Thutmose's workshop.

"If my grandfather had held on to the eye until 1923 when the German revealed he had found the bust, our family would have made millions. Until my grandfather's death he grieved over selling such a valuable relic so cheaply. Mr. Davis would have paid more. He was a very wealthy man." He struggled to his feet. "Now the cursed eye is back in our lives." He limped to the phone. "I'm calling my brother's wife and the police."

Cass motioned toward the front door. We stepped into the street and headed for the van. I checked out every man in a long cotton robe, which was pretty much every man in the market. None looked like a killer who just stabbed a man to death. I also checked out the crowd for a white guy in fancy shoes. There were none. We piled into the van and pulled away from the curb. A police car with strobing blue lights on the roof skidded around the corner and almost ran into us. Alfi slammed on the brakes.

Cass grabbed the dashboard. "Bloody hell! Good driving, my friend." She checked her watch. "Let's talk about next steps. Now we know the eye was in the tomb and Davis didn't find it but wound up buying it from Dharam. Since the eye doesn't show up in Emma's careful records as having been given to the museum, we can deduce Davis kept it in his private collection." She stared out the car window, planning our next move. "Drop us at the Cairo

Museum and meet us tomorrow morning at the hotel across the square."

We jumped the perpetual line of tourists outside the museum with Cass's VIP pass and took the stairs to the basement. She led the way down a narrow main hallway to double doors at the end. The stale air smelled ancient, a combination of dust, mold, and rot. If you breathe the air in the basement long enough like Cass has, you probably become immune to it. I let out a big sneeze.

"Bless you." Cass punched numbers on a keyboard beside the doors and swung them open. The space was pitch black. She switched on lights.

"Wow!" If the windowless room weren't packed from floor to ceiling with boxes on metal shelves, you could have played a football game inside, complete with the cheerleaders and a marching band. Between the rows of shelves, random relics cluttered worktables without any organization as far as I could tell. "How did you find Emma's diaries in here?"

"There is a method to the madness. You have to be able to think as an Egyptian does."

"I'll leave that to you."

"It's this way." In the back near what would have been the opponent's ten-yard line on the football field, she found the right shelf. She climbed a ladder and handed down three boxes marked *Emma Buttles Andrews.*

"What are we looking for exactly?"

"I'm hoping Emma will put us on track from where Mohammed Dharam sold the eye to Davis to where it is now. She kept diaries from age ten until the week before her death in 1922 at eighty-six." She patted the lid of one of the boxes. "They're all here. Emma and Theodore began their relationship in the summer of 1887 at The Reef, the Davis summer home in Newport, Rhode Island. They were both fifty years old. We can start there for context." She made a spot for the boxes on a worktable and opened the middle one. She found the diary marked 1887.

June 10, 1887
The Reef
Newport, Rhode Island

Dear Diary,

I arrived late last night by train via New York City and to my embarrassment overslept this morning, my constitution thinking itself still in Ohio. Cousin Annie is under the weather today, leaving me some blessed time alone to enjoy the balmy breeze off the harbor and to write you.

Do I sound an ungrateful guest in her beautiful new summer home? The estate is an elegant shingle and stone edifice surrounded by walled gardens and acres of meadows dotted with numerous greenhouses. I've not known Cousin Annie to be interested in horticulture. Perhaps it's another hobby of her husband, Cousin Theodore. I peeked into his study at his extensive collection of artifacts from the Orient. I suspect they are quite valuable. I shall ask him at dinner tonight about them as well as the landscape around the estate. Cousin Annie tells me we shall have another guest tonight, a Mister Wetmore. I'm afraid she fancies herself a matchmaker. She told me, not subtly, "We dress for dinner," as though I were her country cousin. She forgets we grew up together in Columbus, Ohio. My upbringing was at least as genteel as her own. Maybe more so.

June 11, 1887
The Reef
Newport, Rhode Island

Dear Diary,

Dinner last night was a rather austere affair, we two ladies in our opera gloves and the men in white tie. Cousin Annie has an air that I can only characterize as sour. Nothing about the service, food, or company seemed pleasing to her. She has two permanent lines between her brows.

Mister Wetmore is the Davis's neighbor, if one can call two estates separated by sixty acres neighbors. He made his fortune, which he is quick to tell one, selling ammunition to both the North and the South during the Great Rebellion. When I hinted such an enterprise might present a moral dilemma, he blinked twice as though the phrase was a new one for him and commented that he saw the transaction as "leveling the table" for the combatants as though he were performing a service. A service to whom I'm not quite sure.

Cousin Theodore was the saving grace of the evening. He is thoroughly delightful, outgoing with a quick wit. He is not a tall person. I always notice height since I'm constantly forced to look up at people, myself being just over five feet. He has a wiry, muscular build with a strong jaw on which he wears muttonchop sideburns in the current fashion. But the most arresting part of his appearance are his eyes, sparkling and alert. He was surprised that I was genuinely interested in his collection of artifacts from the Orient, principally Egypt. In turn he listened raptly when I talked about my passion for providing education opportunities for young women.

After dinner, instead of cigars and brandy for the men and tatting in the sitting room for Cousin Annie and me, Theodore proposed a personal tour of his antiquities collection. I was delighted. Mr. Wetmore stood and straightened his waistcoat and declined, claiming a busy morning the following day. Cousin Annie excused herself to nurse yet another headache.

Theodore and I spent two and a half enchanting hours in his study. He described the provenance of each piece in its custom-built case and each object's significance in the beliefs and daily lives of ancient Egyptian nobility. He says he longs to travel to the country himself and conduct excavations in an area outside Luxor called the Valley of the Kings. He got a far-off look in his eye and *said he imagined the satisfaction of possessing the relics must pale in comparison to the ecstasy of discovering them. The time passed so quickly we both were shocked when the hallway clock chimed midnight. I reluctantly excused myself and left him inspecting a tiny alabaster figure with a magnifying glass. He is altogether a charming and engaging man. I shall cherish the memory of this evening for years to come.*

Cass closed the journal. "The diary documents the obvious two-way attraction between Davis and Emma. They had met in Ohio several times before, but the evening she writes about describes a turning point in her connection with her cousin's husband. Things were pretty grim for intelligent women in her time. Emma was drawn to Davis's passion for his 'hobby' and seduced by his interest in her passion for promoting education for girls."

"Wasn't it unusual for a woman of her class to take up with a married man, especially her cousin's husband?"

"Yes, and they kept up a charade for over twenty years. She moved in at The Reef before the end of the year of this diary entry under the guise of being Cousin Annie's companion. Then she became Cousin Theo's 'traveling companion.' In the winter of 1902, the two made their first trip up the Nile." Cass dug in the box and found the 1902 diary.

December 12, 1902
The Beduin
The Nile River

Dear Diary,
My apologies for ignoring you. The past several days have been a whirlwind. Our ship docked in Alexandria, and we traveled south to Cairo by train. We checked into Shepheard's Hotel awaiting preparation of our boat, The Beduin, *for sailing south to*

Luxor. Shepheard's is the ultimate in elegance. The hotel has luxurious rooms, fine dining, evening orchestra concerts, and a view of the pyramids from an expansive balcony. Anyone who is anyone will stay nowhere else. Our only disappointment was that the hotel was empty. A cholera epidemic has just ended, scaring away less courageous travelers than we.

The boat's outfitting having been completed to Theo's satisfaction, we have been on the river two days relaxing in the quiet of the journey and the ever changing panorama of village life along the river's banks. Our yacht has all the opulence of the house in Newport. The boat is outfitted with a grand piano in the salon, a crystal chandelier in the dining room, a library, four bedrooms (mine is the largest), and bathrooms with tubs. An American flag flies proudly from the stern. The crew of twenty wear matching white turbans and brown cardigans with The Beduin *stitched across the chest.*

Traveling with us are Jones, Theo's valet, and Amelie, my lady's maid. Theo calls his valet Jones the Great because he seems good at everything and mindful of anything that can make life easier for his employer or for me. Theo says when we arrive at Luxor he will employ a dragoman, which is what native guides are called, donkey boys, a dig foreman, and most importantly, an Egyptologist. He means to begin explorations as soon as possible in the Valley of the Kings across the river from Luxor.

Cass closed the book. "He found his first tomb only two months later. Over the next four years he uncovered eighteen tombs. Compare that with the fact that only twenty-five tombs were discovered in the one hundred years before."

"How did he find so many?"

"I think the secret was his temperament as an organizer. Instead of running all over the valley digging holes, he methodically laid out a grid plan and dug to bedrock so as not to miss tombs' entrances. When others were ready to abandon a location, he insisted on sticking to the plan. Also, he was smart enough to hire professional Egyptologists, those who were educated or those who had learned through experience. His ego was healthy. He understood what he was good at and what he wasn't. He visited the digs regularly but left the day-to-day decisions to professionals."

"So he was patient, which is an emotion I'm a long way from feeling right now. Let's get to the clues for how we find the eye."

Cass nodded. She opened the third box. "Let's skip four years ahead to the day they opened KV55—January 9, 1907."

January 9, 1907
The Beduin
The Nile River

Dear Diary,

Mr. Ayrton, Theo's new Egyptologist, has found us a tomb. He is only twenty-five years old and full of energy. He tends to bound rather than walk. For us older folks, the last few days have presented the sensation of occupying the front car on the roller coaster at Coney Island Amusement Park. At least, as I'm told it feels. Slow progress up a steep hill filled with nervous anticipation only to have expectations dashed by a precipitous drop of disappointment. Theo certainly must have been feeling as edgy as I, but he plays the perfect host to our guests on The Beduin *who grow in number every day. My job is to hold court for elite visitors at breakfast, lunch, tea, and dinner. I'll admit to you, Diary, I've spent a great deal of my time during this trip up our beloved Nile waiting for people to leave us and return to the United States or England.*

I shall recount the entire roller-coaster ride of the discovery and opening of Akhenaten's tomb. The first day of the new year, Mr. Ayrton began excavating an enormous heap of limestone chips very near the tomb of Ramses IX. The rubble mound was so close to the Ramses tomb, in fact, that neither Theo nor Ayrton held out much hope of finding a burial site under the debris. After five days digging trenches to the bedrock without any success, Theo was becoming resigned to the idea the effort had been wasted.

On January 6, my niece Mary and her friend Bella arrived from Florence, Italy. Mary is quite an accomplished landscape artist. She was looking forward to capturing on canvas the desert's stark beauty with its singular play of light at dawn and dusk. Her companion Bella is handsome and interesting. She speaks English with the charming tempo and gesticulation of the Italians without any of the self-consciousness some women show when out of their comfort zone.

On January 7, a runner from the dig interrupted our tea with excellent news. Mr. Ayrton had found steps carved into the bedrock. At dawn yesterday the entire company—Theo, Mary, Bella, Jones the valet, and I—boarded donkeys and my "chair" for the trip from the boat to the dig. Jones the Great designed and built my conveyance, a modified carriage on skids to be drawn across the sand by two donkeys.

Our exuberant mood was dashed, however, when we arrived at the dig. Mr. Ayrton had uncovered twelve steps that appeared to lead nowhere. Perhaps a tomb had been begun then quickly abandoned. A plunge in the roller coaster. Then a shout from the bottom of the stairs drew us to the edge of the pit. The foreman had refused to give up. He had uncovered another step.

One more step became nine more leading to a sealed doorway. Behind the first door a second wall of granite blocks was sealed with the official stamp of the guardian of the necropolis, a jackal crouching over nine captives. Theo had found a real tomb. He halted work in order to contact Gaston Maspero, Director General of Egyptian Antiquities Services, as our dig permit requires.

Which brings us, Dear Diary, to this momentous day. After a night when most of us found sleep impossible, this morning,

January 9, the entire party with the addition of Monsieur Maspero trooped again across the sand dunes to witness the tomb's opening. We must have made quite a queer spectacle. Theo led the group riding his favorite donkey he named Anubis after the God of the Underworld. He calls him Noobie for short. Mr. Ayrton and Monsieur Maspero followed astride their own mounts. The ladies—Mary, Bella, I, and Amelie—came next in my chair, and the crew brought up the rear carrying preparations for a formal celebratory lunch at the dig.

Theo was in high spirits. He turned Noobie back down the line to chat and encourage our progress. "Do you have your journal, Emmy? I've a feeling this will be a memorable day."

"I do, Mr. Davis, and Mary has her paints. We are prepared to memorialize this fine day."

He gave me a smile that made the moment special between us and tipped his hat to the other ladies.

When we arrived at the tomb, the way inside had been completely cleared. The large door in the hillside opened into what proved to be a long corridor filled almost to the ceiling with limestone chips and rubble. Theo and Ayrton wriggled and crawled over the rubble through a three-foot gap. Monsieur Maspero's girth being too wide to fit, he and the rest of the party waited outside. At last we heard Theo's voice ring out, "By Jove!" and we knew there must be remarkable things inside.

Cass held the book up to show me. "She begins the detailed inventory of relics taken from the tomb. No mention of the chest and eye. And several pages later she sketched the wall painting in the tomb, the boy offering Akhenaten the chest with Nefertiti's eye."

"So we know now someone found the eye and sold it to Mohammed Dharam and he sold it back to Davis."

"And we know it wasn't included in the KV55 relics Davis transferred to the Cairo Museum. Davis was in the habit of keeping finds in his private collection."

"He wouldn't have felt a responsibility to give the relic to the museum since it came from his dig at KV55?"

"I suspect since he bought the eye from Dharam he wouldn't have hesitated to consider it his personal property."

"So what happened to his private collection?"

Cass opened the third box. "He died in the spring of 1915. Let's see if Emma sheds any light on that." She lifted the 1915 diary from the box and paged through it. "Here it is. She's back in the United States in New York City. On March 18, she writes about attending a reading of Davis's will."

March 18, 1915
Washington Square
New York, New York

Dear Diary,

I have kicked off my shoes, and I'm sipping a peaceful and solitary cup of tea in Mary and Bella's parlor. The trees in Washington Square Park across the street are beginning to sprout their leaves. The joyous cries of children romping around the fountain drift across the street. Mary and Bella are out "giving me my space" after the reading of Theo's last will and testament. In truth, after all the upset of the last few months, today was a relief. A tangible end to our years together. I pray Theo has found rest, though it's difficult to imagine his active and searching mind placid.

Theo's longtime attorney and friend Lucas Conroy having passed away a few years ago, the lawyer's son Lucas Junior presided over the reading in their Wall Street office. Lucas Senior was there in spirit watching over his son's shoulder from a life-sized portrait on the wall behind the young attorney. The formal conference room smelled of the leather chairs and the law books that line the room. Annie was subdued but civil. She is quite feeble, leaning on a cane for support. She won't outlive Theo by much I suspect.

Some provisions of the document will seem odd to outsiders. Theo gave Cousin Annie and me joint occupancy of The Reef as though she and I might live together in the house in harmony after all the water under the bridge. That act makes Theo appear naïve about human nature, which he was not. The ability to read people was the foundation of both his business successes and his achievements in Egypt. He told me once that a business adversary described him as "more cunning than learned and more astute than profound." Theo recounted this description to me with a note of pride in his voice.

The explanation for his decision to link Cousin Annie and me through The Reef is that he expected after his death I would want to keep up the charade of my being her companion. I have no intention of stepping foot again in The Reef.

Another provision will raise eyebrows. Theo has left his most precious possessions—his entire private antiquities collection—to me. Not to his wife, and not to the Museum of Modern Art. He has made a final statement of our love and a gift affirming my contributions to his discoveries. The will shall be probated in three weeks and I have secured a new home for the priceless relics. I've bought a townhouse just down the street from Mary and Bella with a large study to do the treasures justice.

A *thunk* sound interrupted Cass's reading of the diary entry, and the big room went black. "Hey!"

Cass put her finger on my lips. We held our breaths and waited. Someone at the front door switched on a flashlight and swept a slow, wide arc around the room. Cass pulled me out of my chair, and we scrambled in the dark to the end of the aisle of shelves and around the corner.

The flashlight came steadily toward where we were hiding. He stopped and picked up a diary and flipped through a few pages. The light reflected off a gun in his hand. He tossed the book in a box and swept the flashlight beam across the shelves again. We had to do something. I ran my hands blindly over a shelf for anything that could be a weapon. My fingers landed on two heavy objects that felt like softball-sized rocks. He came even with us on the other side of the shelf. Believe it or not, I had to suppress the urge to pee. The situation would have been funny if I hadn't been so terrified.

I stepped around Cass and tossed one of the rocks underhanded past him to his right. The rock clattered against the metal shelving. He turned the flashlight toward the sound. I jumped on his back, rode him to the floor, and hit him with the other rock on the side of the head as hard as I could. He dropped the flashlight and gun and knocked me off his back into the shelving, spilling boxes and relics. He and Cass scrambled after the gun and light, and the guy got to them first. He yelled a threat in Arabic, and she backed away with her hands raised. He pointed the flashlight in her face and yelled again. She helped me to my feet and stood in front of me facing him.

"Where is the eye?" he said in English.

"We don't know."

He grabbed Cass and put her in a chokehold with the gun to her head. "Tell me what you found in the books."

The next things happened in the blink of an eye. The *thunk* sound again, followed by the lights coming on. A shot from the front door. Our assailant falling like a bag of rocks. The front door banging shut. Cass and I looked at each other open-mouthed. She kicked his gun away, which wasn't necessary since the guy died before he hit the floor. He lay on his side with a neat quarter-sized hole in his turban and a dark red halo spreading around his head.

"Look. There's an empty knife scabbard on his belt. I'll bet he killed Mr. Dharam. He's Almafya, right? Who shot him?"

Cass began putting the diaries into their boxes. "Somebody with really good aim. Help me put these boxes away. We need to leave. People will have heard the disturbance."

I climbed the ladder and stacked the boxes as she handed them up, then climbed down. "Someone keeps saving us."

"He's letting us do the work of finding the eye so he can step in and claim it."

"Helga and the Hitler Youth people?"

"Maybe. We need to follow the trail to New York. We're very close. We'll fly out right away."

"What about our stuff in Luxor?"

"Alfi will get our KV55 discoveries to the museum. Sam the hotel manager can make arrangements for our bags to be delivered to my hotel in New York." She pointed to the rock I hit the guy on the head with. "Taweret watched over us."

I picked up the granite carving of a hippopotamus. "Taweret?"

"She's a protective goddess." She wrapped her arms around me. "That was quick thinking on your part."

I felt a tingle of pleasure at her compliment. "I'm not sure it's thinking. More reflex." I put Taweret on a shelf. "What's the next step?"

"Emma inherited Davis's collection. The eye must have been part of it. Emma died in 1922. We need to find the next link in the chain…who Emma left the collection to. We need someone in New York to help find the name of Emma's heir." Cass pulled the cocktail napkin with Pia's phone number from her pocket. She had been carrying the napkin around as if she knew we'd need it. "Pia must be back in New York by now. I'll call her and see if she'll meet us at the Plaza when we get to town."

Chapter Twelve

CASS WAS SITTING DEEP in concentration at a table under the domed leaded glass roof of the Palm Court off the lobby in the Plaza Hotel. She bit the end of her pen and then wrote something in her journal. I stood for a moment behind a palm watching her. She's the kind of person who is as comfortable in the tearoom of a fancy hotel as she is on her hands and knees digging in the dirt for pottery shards. Do you have to be born with that temperament, or is it something you can learn? She glanced up and saw me and made a little wave.

The maître d' gave me the once-over from my bright yellow knit beanie to my penny loafers. "Yes, madam?"

I pointed across the room. "I'm with her."

He made a little bow. "Of course." He led me to the table and pulled out a chair. "Your server will be right over." He bustled off.

"Hello, darling. I've ordered afternoon tea. I skipped lunch and I'm starving. But you have whatever you like. I wish you'd change your mind and stay here at the Plaza with me."

"If I'm going to keep my job at Barnard after the holidays, I need to spend time at the dorm and attend some meetings. The floor counselors have to go through orientation before each semester."

"I'm sorry things are a bit up in the air right now. We'll have them sorted out as soon as we find the eye. We're so close." She put her hand on mine. "Can't you stay with me tonight?"

"You know I want to, but sometimes I get uncomfortable about you paying for everything."

"I've never had to think about money, and I'll admit that can make me insensitive about how other people obsess about it."

That was annoying. "I wouldn't say I obsess."

She took a sip of tea and smoothed the napkin on her lap. I got the distinct impression she'd rather talk about anything but this. I pressed on. "Paying for everything can be a way to have power over someone."

"Oh, Ari, I'm not trying to control you. Far from it."

"You've never told me anything about where your money comes from. For example, who finances your digs? And where do you live when you're not staying in some hotel?"

"I'm not being mysterious on purpose or trying to have control over you—" Cass interrupted herself pointing toward the front. "Here's Pia now."

Pia was bundled up in a green wool coat with a fur collar and leather gloves. The color of her coat set off her striking red hair. After she settled and we both ordered tea, she bounced in her seat. "I'm so excited. Can we get started?"

Cass turned to a clean page in her journal. "By all means, let's begin."

Pia opened a file folder. "The clues from Emma's diary you supplied on the phone gave me a starting point. The main characters are Theodore Davis, his wife Anna Buttles Davis, Emma Buttles Andrews, Emma's niece Mary Buttles, and Mary's companion Bella Donatello. My first stop was the *New York Times* morgue. It's a fascinating place. If you've never been there..."

Cass and I both shook our heads.

"You must go some time. It's three stories below the street, dark and quiet except for the occasional rumbling of the subway. Perfect for a researcher like me. Hardly anyone from the public goes there. The staff clip, index, and physically save every article written in the *Times* going back to the 1870s. There are hundreds of thousands of articles stored in steel filing cabinets. You would think by the looks that it's all a big jumble, but they have a system. They can find whatever you're looking for if what you seek is important or interesting enough to have made the newspaper."

The server brought finger sandwiches and scones and poured our tea.

"Don't let me go on too long. I'm very excited as you can tell. From the diary we know Theodore left Emma his private antiquities collection. You described her buying a home near Washington Square Park to house the collection just after Theodore's will was read. That would have been in 1915. She lived seven more years. I've copied her obituary." She handed Cass a Xerox page, and Cass leaned near me so I could follow along as Pia read.

January 19, 1922

Emma Buttles Andrews of this city passed away peacefully in her sleep at the age of 84. She was preceded in death by her parents, Joel Buttles and Lauretta Barnes Buttles, and ten brothers and sisters.

Mrs. Andrews served as honorary treasurer of the Newport, Rhode Island branch of the Egypt Exploration Fund. She accompanied her cousin, Theodore M. Davis, on seventeen trips to Luxor, Egypt on which she served as official record keeper for Mr. Davis's many successful expeditions.

In 1889, Mrs. Andrews founded the Newport Industrial School for Girls.

She is survived by her beloved niece, Mary Neil Buttles. Interment will be at Rose Lawn Cemetery in Columbus, Ohio following a private service.

Pia looked up. "By the way, before we start throwing bouquets at Emma for founding a girls' school, I researched this particular institution, a reform school for so-called delinquent girls. Newport Industrial School for Girls was notorious for physical and sexual abuse of girls it claimed to 'reform, educate, and reintroduce as productive adults.'"

Cass made a note in her journal. "No mention of Emma's husband and son, both dead. The article lists only one survivor, Mary. Emma's diary mentions Mary and her companion Bella being present in the Valley of the Kings when Davis opened Akhenaten's tomb. Also in the entry about the Davis will reading she describes staying at Mary and Bella's home."

Pia nodded. "After the *Times* morgue I went to Surrogate Court down on Chester Street. They handle probate of all wills. I found Emma's." She passed Cass a stapled packet. "To save you reading through the entire document, she left the antiquities collection to her niece Mary. While I was at the court I checked for Mary's will, not knowing if she has passed. The search was trickier since I was working without a date. Turns out she died in 1955."

She handed Cass a slim packet of two or three pages. "Mary left all her assets including the Davis collection and a townhouse at 19 Washington Square North to Bella Donatello. The only other beneficiary was their housekeeper Frances Archer. Mary left the maid a three hundred dollar a month allowance for life. I didn't find a will for Bella and she's listed in the current phone book at the Washington Square address, so I figure she's still alive."

Cass's hands shook as she thumbed through Mary's will. If there hadn't been a table between Pia and her, she would have embraced the redhead. Instead, she took her hand. "Brilliant."

Pia's cheeks colored. "That means so much coming from you."

I'm not proud to confess I felt a flash of irrational anger and a desire to discredit Pia's research somehow. The jealousy rearing its head. Of course the information she had found was terrific. I hugged myself to get control. "We've come all this way, and the Queen's eye may be waiting on Bella Donatello's bookshelf in Greenwich Village."

Chapter Thirteen

DURING THE NIGHT AFTER our meeting with Pia, a January storm dumped eight inches of snow on Manhattan, snarling morning rush hour traffic. The plows trying to clear the streets only made things worse.

"How do you feel about walking the rest of the way to Washington Square?" Cass and I got out of the taxi at the Flatiron Building where Fifth Avenue and Broadway cross to form a giant X. Cass put her arm through mine, and we started south.

Manhattan was waking up and going about its business. Shopkeepers shoveled snow to clear the sidewalks in front of their doors. Delivery van drivers double-parked and hauled out their loads. Occasionally a taxi honked halfheartedly in a futile attempt to move traffic along. "How did Bella Donatello sound on the phone? What did you tell her about your reason for calling? Did she seem open to seeing us or reluctant?"

"Before I introduced myself, she sounded cautious, of course, as anyone would with a call from a stranger out of the blue. I introduced myself as a Columbia professor. She recognized my name from the Hatshepsut discovery. She was very knowledgeable and complimentary about that. I told her we are working on solving another ancient mystery, and we think she might be important to the answer. That's when she agreed to see us this morning. She sounds pleasant with her charming Italian accent." She hugged my arm close to her side. "I can hardly believe we're about to gaze upon Nefertiti's eye. Right here in New York City."

"You're that confident?"

"I have a feeling."

Fifth Avenue dead ends at Washington Square Park. When Emma wrote in her diary about putting up her feet and sipping her tea across from the park in 1915, she said the season was spring. She wrote that the trees were starting to bud, and she heard the squeals of children playing around the fountain. On the winter morning when Cass and I reached the park it was blanketed in white. We stopped a minute to watch kids building a giant snowman.

I tightened the knot on the scarf around my neck. "I love this park. It's pretty even in winter."

"Do you know its past? The area was originally a potter's field, a burial place for people too poor to buy their own graves. The town also used the space for public executions. That big elm tree is nicknamed Hangman's Elm."

"Oh, my God, Cass. Sometimes there is such a thing as knowing too much history. From now on I'll never see just a pretty park. I'll always picture gallows and tombstones."

"Sorry. It's the scientist in me."

Nineteen Washington Square North is a three-story building in a row of immaculately restored townhouses across the street and north of the George Washington tribute arch. We opened the wrought iron gate and climbed four steps. Cass pushed the button and a bell sounded inside. An older woman in a black high-necked dress with a starched white collar opened the door. Her hair was pulled back in a tight bun. I figured this was Frances Archer, the housekeeper mentioned in Mary's will. "Dr. Stillwell?"

"Yes, and this is my colleague, Ari Morgan."

"Miss Donatello is waiting for you in the parlor."

Bella Donatello rose to greet us. She was tall. Her dark, naturally curly hair was cut short and sprinkled with gray. Her slim, tan wool skirt and light blue sweater flattered her trim figure. She was a handsome woman with features too strong to be called pretty. "Good morning, Dr. Stillwell. Please come in. I have some coffee waiting for us. And who is this charming young lady?" Like Cass said, a lilting Italian accent colored her perfect English.

I felt my familiar urge to stand up straighter and tuck in my shirt.

Cass put out her hand. "Please call me Cass, and this is Ari Morgan, Miss Donatello."

She smiled at me and took Cass's hand in both hers. "Call me Bella, please." She gestured toward a sofa. "Sit."

The housekeeper straightened a shawl around Bella's shoulders and poured our coffee. "If there's nothing more, I'll leave you to your visitors."

"Thank you, Mrs. Archer." Bella looked at Cass. "You are here about Nefertiti's eye. That's the ancient mystery you mentioned on the phone."

Cass didn't miss a beat. "Yes."

"Mary told me this day would come. She didn't know the seeker would be you, of course. You must have been just beginning your illustrious career when she left us in 1955."

"I was still an undergraduate."

Bella stirred her coffee. "Do you want to know our story?"

"We'd be honored."

"Mary inherited the eye in 1922 from her Aunt Emma along with the rest of Theodore Davis's private collection of Egyptian relics. The eye in its lovely little chest was one of many fine pieces. The Met immediately began courting her to donate the collection. Their attentions almost overwhelmed us. The director, Mr. Robinson, was quite persistent. We were offered opera and ballet tickets and use of the Met's Philharmonic box seats. He proposed naming a gallery for displaying the collection after Aunt Emma. Mary was still grieving Emma's passing and she simply wasn't ready to make a decision. Then in 1923, we and the rest of the world learned the significance of the eye when Mr. Borchardt announced his discovery in the ruins of Thutmose's workshop— Nefertiti's bust missing her left eye, the Germans installing her in their fancy museum in Berlin, and all the rest of it. Borchardt's theory was that the bust was a model and the eye never existed, but of course we knew better."

Cass nodded and patiently sipped her coffee. I wanted to yell, *We know the story already. Can we see the eye?*

"At the time, Mary and I were busy with our lives. We were still maintaining the villa in Florence and spending several months a year there, but we became more and more nervous about politics in Italy and in Europe in general. In 1936, Mussolini and Hitler signed their little love pact, their military alliance. We began making plans to emigrate permanently to the United States. Then, Hitler invaded Poland in 1939. We sold the villa and never returned to our beloved Florence."

"Who knew about your having the eye?"

"No one knew the specifics of what items made up Theodore's collection. The Met pressed her to allow an inventory, but Mary was determined to keep the eye a secret during the war. After Hitler fell, she hoped Egypt would negotiate Nefertiti's return to Cairo. She closely followed the talks back and forth. She not only inherited Emma's estate but also her love for Egypt. At times she felt elated when negotiations appeared to be progressing, then depressed as things fell apart. At one point, Hitler personally intervened to put a stop to the deal." Bella sighed heavily and shook her head. "My Mary didn't live to see an agreement."

Cass opened her bag. "I want to show you something, Bella." She brought out the papyrus and moved her coffee cup to make a space to unfurl it. Thutmose's blueprint was as much a remarkable work of art in its own way as the bust itself.

Bella gasped and touched her throat. "Look at her with both her eyes. It's as though she's about to speak." She moved closer to study the papyrus. "Where did you find this?"

"In Akhenaten's tomb, KV55, just a few days ago."

"Mary and I were there in 1907 the day Theodore opened the tomb." She ran a finger over the papyrus. "Theodore left this treasure behind? How is that possible?"

"Someone in antiquity hid the papyrus and eye in the burial chamber. We found a clue in Emma's diary, and we were lucky to follow the clue and find the papyrus." She pulled from her bag the Xerox page with Emma's sketch of the wall painting. "This drawing from the diary provided a hint that led us to open the tomb and dig in the burial chamber. That's where we found the papyrus, but we found no eye. Do you remember seeing the wall painting in the tomb?"

Bella picked up a little silver bell from beside her coffee cup and rang it. Frances Archer popped into the room. She must have been hovering around the corner listening to our conversation. "Mrs. Archer, take Cass and Ari upstairs to my bedroom and show them the watercolors."

"Certainly." The housekeeper led us through the foyer to a staircase. Cass ran her hand lightly over the ornately carved cap of the newel post. "This is a beautiful home. Remarkable woodwork."

"Thank you. Miss Bella is very proud of it." I picked up a note of possessive pride in Mrs. Archer's voice. She was clearly proud of the house too. "The house was built in 1829." She led us up the stairs to the second floor and into Bella's bedroom. Large windows across one wall overlooked the park. Three watercolors hung on the opposite wall. "Miss Mary painted these during their trip to Luxor in 1907."

The one on the left was a portrait of a young Bella. Her black hair was minus the gray and longer than she kept it now, curled on her shoulders. She wore a wide-brimmed straw hat and wire-rimmed sunglasses. She gazed past the artist with a small smile on her lips that reminded me of Nefertiti's bust. The portrait hinted at a subject and an artist very much in the throes of a new love. The second painting was a landscape looking from the east bank across the Nile toward the green line of date palms on the west bank. Feluccas like Omar's drifted across the placid water along the near shore. The third painting was a detailed image of the tomb painting in Akhenaten's burial chamber.

Mrs. Archer led us back downstairs to the parlor. Cass took a seat across from Bella and leaned forward with her elbows on her knees. "The watercolors are beautiful. They illustrate Mary's deep appreciation for her subjects."

"It was her first trip to Egypt and our first journey together. We had known each other only a few weeks." She got a far-off look in her eye. "It was magical." She sipped her coffee. "Mary was older than I and well-traveled in Europe and the United States when we met in Florence. I had never traveled farther away than Rome and Naples. Egypt enchanted her from that very first trip. Having the vision of a painter, she was mesmerized by the special quality of the light and the ever changing panorama of life on the shores of the Nile."

"And you?"

Bella chuckled. "I blush to recall how much I missed during the trip. I felt a little jealous of her attention to her Aunt Emma. I was self-absorbed, as the young can be. Mary and I might as well have been on the Arno flowing through the middle of Florence instead of on the Nile. I hope over the years of my life with her, some of her awareness and appreciation of the world around us rubbed off."

"But you must remember entering the tomb that day in 1907?"

"Yes, and I remember the painting on the wall. Clearly it made an impression on Mary too. Before seeing your papyrus, I certainly didn't realize the painting's significance and its connection to Nefertiti."

"Now you are the keeper of her eye."

"Yes. It rests securely in a wall safe in my study down the hall." She tapped her lips with a manicured finger. "What do you want from this treasure, Dr. Stillwell? To increase your already considerable fame? Or is your desire for money?" Bella was asking whether Cass was a graverobber.

I held my breath for a strong reaction from Cass. She folded her hands and paused. "I want to see Nefertiti made whole and returned to Cairo. Borchardt took the bust from Thutmose's workshop to Germany under false pretenses for personal gain and hid her from the world for ten years. His motive was to impress his financial backer and a chauvinistic desire to keep her for Germany. From what you've said, if Mary were here with you today, I believe she and I would find common cause."

Bella pulled in a heavy breath. Her voice broke. "If only she were here."

Cass leaned to the edge of her seat. "With your possession of the eye and my connections in the archaeology world, we may have the leverage to accomplish the repatriation Mary wished for."

Bella rose and went to gaze out the window toward the park. The kids were placing the head on the body to complete their snowman. Bella said, "I'll think about it."

"Thank you. Am I too forward asking you to tea at the Plaza tomorrow to discuss my proposal further?"

"I think that would be fine." She smiled at Cass, then me, and put her hand on my arm and gave a little squeeze. If I didn't know better, I'd say she was flirting.

"Good. The Palm Court at four."

Mrs. Archer showed us out. We started toward the corner of Fifth Avenue to catch a cab. I looked back over my shoulder at the housekeeper still standing at the open door watching us. "She gives me the creeps."

"Who? Bella?"

"No, the housekeeper. Didn't you notice she hovered over our conversation with Bella the whole time?"

"She certainly seems devoted to her employer."

The snowplows had cleared the roads and traffic was moving like a normal rush hour. "I think Bella will join you in your mission to get the bust back to Egypt."

"I'm optimistic." She glanced at me sideways. "I noticed she was quite taken with you. That can't hurt our cause."

"She's very attractive. Maybe I remind her of Mary." A taxi threw up a rooster tail of slush that barely missed dousing us. "But assuming Bella works with us, we still have to overcome Germany's objections to the repatriation." I got a picture of the six feet and icy eyes of Helga von Halle standing in the middle of the ruins of Neues Museum in Berlin declaring, *Your countries divided our homeland. Someday the Wall will come down, and the German people will be one again. Then Nefertiti's home can be restored.*

I glanced at Cass. "I know you're optimistic, but if Helga von Halle is an indication, what we've overcome to find the eye might look like a day on the beach compared with what we'll encounter getting Nefertiti back to Egypt. We've been almost kidnapped, shot at, and nearly hijacked on the road. We shouldn't get overly confident."

"I appreciate your natural skepticism, but let in the possibility of a favorable outcome. People will often do the right thing." She touched the gold necklace she always wore. "When I was young, I had a good role model for optimism."

"You mean your special friend Jessie at Oxford who gave you that necklace. You haven't mentioned her since that first night in Luxor, but I can tell she's often in your thoughts."

"Yes, she is."

I suspected she wanted to say, *As Mary is in Bella's thoughts.*

We walked along in silence for a while. I waited for more about her friend who died of breast cancer, but Cass shifted the conversation back to the bust. "Don't assume the German people are all ultra-nationalists like the ones who are chasing us. The

Minister for Arts and Antiquities in Berlin was very accommodating."

"Did you tell him why we were interested in the bust?"

"Not in so many words."

"Right. I'm just saying, even with Bella's cooperation and the eye as a bargaining chip, Germany giving up Nefertiti will be over Helga's dead body and other people like her."

The kids building Mr. Snowman were putting finishing touches on his face, pieces of coal for the eyes and a carrot for the nose. A small crowd had gathered to watch. Something about one of the watchers caught my attention. He passed his hand over his salt-and-pepper hair then turned and walked quickly south.

"Cass, the guy from Berlin. The shoe guy! He was in the crowd by the snowman. He headed off that way through the park, walking fast."

"What? Are you sure?"

"Well, almost sure. He's followed us to New York. What if we led him straight to Bella and the eye?"

She grabbed my hand, and we ran across the street, under the memorial arch, and around the fountain. The path was icy, so it was slow going. We ran through the park and stopped for breath at the south edge.

I looked up and down the sidewalk paralleling Washington Square South. No sign of him in either direction. "He must have kept going straight south on Thompson. I'm almost sure it was him. We may have led him to Bella. What if we've put her in danger? Don't we have to warn her? We should call the police."

"This may have been the best thing that could happen."

"Okay, that's beyond optimistic. What are you thinking?"

"Suspecting we've located the whereabouts of the eye may smoke him out in the open. We can learn who is behind these attacks on us."

"Do you mean we should hide and try to nab him in the act of stealing the eye?" I remembered crouching in the dark in Cass's bedroom at the Winter Palace Hotel a few months before. Cass had the big idea of catching the thief of Hatshepsut's crystal red-handed. That little escapade ended with a murder in the sitting room of our suite and a whole go-around with the Luxor police. I certainly didn't want a repeat of that episode. "I think we should involve NYPD. What if something happens to Bella because we're playing detective? We already know these people can be ruthless."

"Here are the problems." Cass counted them off on her fingers. "First, they haven't actually committed a crime here in the US."

"Not yet."

"Second, I suspect the man who's been following us will have some kind of diplomatic cover. He doesn't appear to be your average criminal type."

"You didn't see him rolling around on the floor of the sleeper car and hear him throw the guy off the train. He's plenty criminal for my taste."

"True, but I'd really like to catch him in the act. We'd know exactly what we're up against."

I gave one more look up and down the sidewalk. There was no sign of him. "It's one thing if we choose to pretend to be Sherlock Holmes and Dr. Watson, but we shouldn't jeopardize Bella's safety."

"We can let Bella participate in the decision. She doesn't seem a shrinking violet type to me, but you're right. She should have all the facts as we know them. We'll tell her the whole story at tea tomorrow. Then we can decide about the police." Cass had already turned around and started back toward Fifth Avenue to hail a cab. I ran to catch up.

* * * * *

The following afternoon, the maître d' at the Palm Court recognized Bella Donatello and couldn't stop giving her obsequious little bows as he led her to our table. He took her fur coat and held her chair. "A pleasure to see you again, Miss Donatello. Your server will be right over."

Bella leaned across the table and whispered. "Mary and I used to come here often after shopping on winter days like this. She was a notoriously big tipper, which explains the overzealous bowing and scraping. I apologize for the show." She leaned back. "Now down to business. You're proposing I offer the Germans Nefertiti's eye in exchange for their agreement to give her back to Egypt."

Cass reached across the table and put her hand on Bella's. "Before you decide, there's been another development we must tell you about. To put events in context..." Cass began the narrative of the last few weeks. Could it have been only a few weeks?

She described finding Emma's diaries in the basement of the Cairo Museum with her sketch of the only tomb painting in KV55. "I had read the many accounts of Borchardt's discovering the bust several years after Davis opened KV55, including his firsthand narrative, and his theory that the sculptor deliberately left one eye missing. I've always suspected Borchardt's exploration of Thutmose's ancient workshop was hasty. His motives appeared more to do with currying favor with his wealthy patron and achieving recognition for Germany."

The server interrupted with our tea accompanied by more bowing and hovering by the maître d'.

Cass got back to the story. "Our visit to Berlin to see Nefertiti in person set off a chain of events. On the positive side, they have led us to you and the eye. On the negative, our efforts to find the missing eye have attracted the attention of some dangerous people."

I studied Bella's face for a reaction, concern or alarm. She nodded and stirred her tea. "Go on."

"In Egypt, we encountered antiquities thieves called Almafya who saw the eye as a treasure that could command a fortune on the black market. In a way, they were the more manageable threat because their motives were straightforward. I'm fairly sure we left them behind in Egypt. But there are other forces at work here in New York that may pose a more complicated threat."

"What forces?"

"Are you familiar with the National Identity Underground in Germany?"

"I've heard of them, but I wouldn't say I'm familiar. Once Mary and I settled in the United States and the war was won, we truly left Europe behind."

"They are zealots who wish to restore their idea of the former glory of the Third Reich. In our case, they've focused on keeping Nefertiti in Germany as emblematic of the 'dignity, pride, and grandeur' of the whole country. Thankfully, their views represent a tiny minority in Germany. I believe that with the prospect of restoring the missing eye, the Minister of Arts and Antiquities, Lothar Stoph, will be open to discussing repatriation of Nefertiti to Egypt where I believe she belongs."

"You said the National Identity Underground are dangerous. How dangerous?"

Cass cleared her throat. I could imagine what she was thinking. She was trying the words out in her head. *There have been two murders that we know of and several encounters involving guns. Now we may have led them to your door.* I hoped she wouldn't try and sugarcoat it.

"They're armed and determined. They followed us from Berlin to Egypt, and we suspect we may have led them to you and the eye here in New York. Ari caught sight of one of them in the park yesterday as we were leaving your house."

This time Bella did react. "Hmm." She looked at me, then back at Cass. "Have you contacted the police?"

Cass scooted to the edge of her seat. "I'd like you to understand. I wanted to keep the police out of the situation in Egypt because I didn't know whom we could trust, and I thought we were close to finding the eye in KV55. I was concerned the authorities getting involved would jeopardize the discovery."

I jumped in. "We did tell the Luxor detective after Almafya shot a dig worker." I didn't want Bella to think we were completely reckless about the threat to our safety and those around us.

Cass carried on. "Until the NIU make a move here in New York, I believe we'd have a difficult time convincing the New York police to pay attention. But if we can lure the NIU operative into trying to steal the eye..."

"Do you mean lure him into my home and catch him in the act?"

"Yes."

I held my breath and waited for Bella to push up from her chair and tell Cass she must have lost her mind. I was shocked when she said, "Tell me how we would do that." Cass had pegged her right. She was no shrinking violet.

Chapter Fourteen

THE WHOLE DAY HAD been gloomy. At 7:15 the sky was pitch dark when the cab dropped us on the street behind Bella's townhouse north of Washington Square. Clouds covered a sliver of a moon. Cass flicked her cigarette lighter and checked her watch. "We're a little early. It will give us time to get settled before she leaves." She tried the latch on the gate and found it unlocked. "So far, so good."

The gate swung open to a small garden with patches of dormant grass and hedges peeking through a cover of snow. Bella had drawn us a little map showing the back entrance to the basement with helpful comments like "I've left the basement door unlocked with the key inside in the keyhole." and "Open the door slowly. The hinges creak if they haven't been oiled recently." Once Cass got Bella on board with the plan to catch the Berlin guy stealing the eye, she really got into the swing of things. I was worried they were both treating the whole situation like an adventure, ignoring the risk.

Cass whispered, "Turn on the torch, but turn it off as soon as we're inside." I flicked on the heavy police-sized flashlight I picked up at the army and navy store down the street from Columbia. I counted on using it as a weapon if necessary. I followed Cass into the basement, a chilly open space the size of the footprint of the first floor. Once I switched off the flashlight, the only illumination in the room came from a streetlight through a small window that gave a ground-level view of the street in front of the house.

When my eyes adjusted to the dim interior, I could make out shelves filled with neatly arranged storage boxes lining two walls, a furnace against a third, and stairs leading up to the first floor of the house on the fourth wall. The sound of Bella's voice drifted down the stairwell. "I'll be gone only the one night, Frances. Are you sure you won't change your mind and use the opportunity to visit your sister in New Jersey?"

"No, ma'am. I've started a good mystery. I'll go upstairs early and put my feet up and read."

I sucked in a breath. The housekeeper being home presented a complication we hadn't planned for. Cass put her finger to my lips to shush me.

Bella again. "If I didn't expect the gala to run late I'd plan to come home, but you never know how long winded these society types will be. Everyone has to have his fifteen minutes in the spotlight. Here's my car now. I'll be at the Pierre. Home for breakfast at the usual time."

"Yes, Miss Bella."

The front door opened then clicked shut. We watched Bella go down the steps to the street carrying an overnight bag. She glanced over her shoulder at the basement window then climbed in the back seat of a black Lincoln town car. The car pulled away from the curb.

Cass whispered in my ear. "We may be in for a long wait. If he's watching from across the street as I suspect, he'll let some time go by."

"How do you know he'll show up?"

"I have a feeling."

We sat on the bottom step of the stairs, and Cass unfolded a blanket she'd brought and draped it across our laps. The stairs from the first to the second floor creaked above our heads—Mrs. Archer going up to read her book like she said.

"You're shaking. Are you warm enough?" Cass put her arm around my shoulders and pulled me close. A lump in her coat pocket pressed hard against my thigh.

I scooted away a little. "I still think that gun is a bad idea."

"We won't have to use it. We'll take him by surprise. It's insurance." Her voice was steady and confident. "Here, I'll move it to a different pocket. Better?" Then she said, "I wish I had a cigarette." A dead giveaway she was nervous too.

I tried to make out her face in the gloom. "Right after this we're going to the police, no matter what reservations you have."

"Fine."

We leaned into each other, and Cass tucked the blanket around our legs. I must have drifted off. When the doorbell rang, I jumped a mile. Cass went to the window and stood on tiptoes to peer out. She turned and shook her head and mouthed "Can't see."

The bell rang again. The housekeeper's hurried footsteps sounded on the stairs above us. "Coming, coming." The front door opened, then silence. I guessed Berlin guy was pointing a gun in the housekeeper's face. I started up the basement stairs with my flashlight, but Cass held me back and whispered. "Give him a minute to find the study. We want to catch him in the act of stealing the eye. And leave that gigantic torch here. It'll only be in the way." She stepped around me and pulled the gun from her pocket.

We climbed the stairs, and she opened the basement door a crack and listened. Still no sound from Mrs. Archer or the guy. I followed Cass into the dark entryway. Down the hall, the door to the study where Bella kept Nefertiti's eye was open. A yellow square of light fell across the hardwood floor. Murmur of a woman's voice. I pictured Mrs. Archer bound hand and foot at the mercy of the Berlin guy. We crept down the hallway hugging the wall. Cass reached back to squeeze my hand. Was that to reassure me or herself? She stepped into the room.

At first, the two people didn't notice us. There was no sign of Mrs. Archer. Berlin guy stood with his back to the door looking over the shoulder of a blond woman with her face close to the combination dial of a wall safe. The woman was Helga von Halle! Berlin guy rocked back and forth impatiently while Helga ticked the wheel forward, backward, then forward again. She tried the lever. The safe didn't open. She rattled the lever and muttered under her breath in German, "Scheisse, scheisse, scheisse."

Cass pointed the gun at Helga's back and took a step forward. "Put your hands on your heads and turn around slowly."

Helga whirled around at the sound of Cass's voice and went for a gun lying on the desk. Cass pulled the trigger. The gunshot thundered in the small space, and a leather blotter on the desk flew straight up in the air and came down with a baseball-sized hole in the middle. I instinctively yelled, "Hey!" and jumped back a step. I was pretty sure Bella didn't expect to have her home shot up when she agreed to this escapade.

"Sit." Cass motioned with the gun barrel to a chair behind the desk. "Helga, you there, and you, there."

The guy stuck his hands in the air and dropped down in a side chair, but Helga hesitated. Cass took another step toward her. "I won't miss."

Helga sat behind the desk.

"Get the gun, Ari."

I scooped Helga's pistol off the desktop and glanced at Cass. The gun in her hand was perfectly steady and the set of her shoulders said she was in charge of things.

Helga leaned back in the leather chair as though this were a perfectly normal business discussion. "You don't want to escalate this situation, Dr. Stillwell. My colleague Gunther and I are merely claiming what should have been a part of Borschadt's glorious discovery in the first place. Nefertiti and Germany deserve the completion the eye will provide. Our people shielded her through the Allied invasion of our country, hid her in banks and churches and salt mines, and now protect her in her inadequate, tiny museum. She will be restored to glory after the Wall finally comes down."

I was beginning to worry Cass would let Helga rave on forever about the majesty of the Fatherland while in the meantime the housekeeper was bleeding to death somewhere. I jumped in. "What have you done with Mrs. Archer?"

Helga gave a chilling smirk. Someone shoved me from behind into Cass's side, and she stumbled and landed sprawled across the desk. She lost her grip on the gun, and it slid across the ruined blotter into Helga's lap. I dropped Helga's pistol I had picked up off the desk, and when it hit the floor it accidently went off, shattering the shade of a Tiffany lamp across the room. Helga grabbed Cass's gun from her lap and pointed it at us.

Gunther picked up Helga's pistol from the floor and put a restraining hand on her arm. He said a few words in German. Helga relaxed a little but kept the gun trained on Cass.

Mrs. Archer stood in the open doorway behind us with her hands on her hips. "I gave you the combination, and I just saved your bacon, so now I need to get paid." She had shoved me into Cass. She was in league with Helga. I had a gut feeling all along we couldn't trust her.

Helga paced behind the desk. "The combination you gave us doesn't work. If you want to get paid, you'd better find some way of opening this safe."

"Try it again. That's got to be right." She shoved me aside and stepped in front of the safe. She spun the wheel back and forth. It didn't open. "Damn! The old biddy must have changed the combination without telling me. Typical. And I should have suspected she'd get these two involved." She checked her watch. "She'll be home early in the morning. You can force the combination out of her."

Helga came around the desk and started for the door. "Unless we can find the new combination, our only choice will be to wait for her. I'm going to check the street. Someone may have heard the gunshots and called the police. Gunther, you find rope and secure these two in the basement while I come up with a new plan." She pointed to the ruined desk blotter and the shards of broken glass from the lampshade. "Mrs. Archer, you straighten this place up and search for the new combination. Maybe she wrote it down somewhere."

Gunther herded Cass and me through the foyer and down the basement steps. He found some folding chairs and a coil of cotton clothesline on a shelf. He unfolded two chairs and pointed to one. "Sit."

Cass stepped in front of me. "Your name is Gunther is it?"

He didn't respond.

"Why do you keep saving us, Gunther? You rescued Ari from Almafya on the train, and you shot our assailant in the museum basement, right?"

He pointed at me then motioned to a chair. "Sit."

Cass kept at him. "I understand enough German to know you stopped Helga shooting me just now. I suspect you're having reservations about this whole affair."

I was afraid she'd rile him up and make things worse. We weren't exactly holding a strong hand. I plopped down in the chair. He secured my legs then pulled my arms behind me and looped the rope around them. While he was focusing on tying the knot, Cass launched herself at him. She knocked me and the chair and Gunther to the floor. He managed to hold on to his gun, and he scrambled to his feet and stuck the barrel to my temple. "Back up and sit down or you'll force me to shoot her."

Cass raised her hands and sat.

Gunther righted my chair with me in it and finished the knots on my hands and feet, then tied up Cass. "If you're as smart as you think you are, you'll keep quiet and let this play itself out." He gave our ropes a last check and stomped up the stairs.

I squirmed against the knots to see if there was any wiggle room. They were tight. "What did he mean, play itself out?"

"I don't know what he meant, but what's important now is finding some way to warn Bella. She's walking straight into a trap. I'm going to maneuver closer to you. If we can get back-to-back maybe you can untie my hands." She began scooting her chair toward mine inch by inch. She was making progress when the door at the top of the stairs opened, and Frances Archer came down.

She sat on the bottom step. "Helga sent me to watch you till the old lady shows up. I suppose you're judging me right now. I never meant things to go this far. It's all Miss Bella's fault. If she hadn't got the two of you involved and then changed the combination, they'd be out of here and gone with the eye, and I'd be where you are, tied up to make it look like they got the jump on me. Not to mention I'd be considerably richer."

Cass struggled against the ropes around her wrists. "You don't want to do this, Mrs. Archer. It isn't going to end well, and it's not too late to change things. You can untie us."

For a second, Archer seemed to actually be calculating whether to let us go. I watched her run through an internal dialogue, tilting her head first to one side then the other. "Those two upstairs aren't exactly master criminals from what I can see." She made a decision. "Judge me all you want. Those two old lezzies, Miss Mary and Miss Bella, treated me like dirt for years. All the money Miss Mary had, and she leaves me a lousy three hundred dollars a month. It serves them right if Helga takes their precious eye."

"If it's about money, I'll pay you double what they've promised."

"Double." She sniffed. "How do I know you'll come through with the money? Unless you're carrying around five thousand dollars in your pocket."

"You can keep my necklace as collateral."

I squirmed in the folding chair. "Cass! Don't do that. You can't trust her to give it back."

Archer sidled over to Cass. "Let me see this necklace."

Cass brushed her collar aside with her chin.

Archer lifted Hatshepsut's cartouche on her fingertip. The diamond sparkled even in the dim interior of the cellar. She leaned in, nose to nose with Cass. "This must be a real diamond. You're too hoity-toity to wear a rhinestone."

"Yes, it's real."

Archer barked a laugh in Cass's face. "Do you think I'm a fool? If I untie you now, you call the police, Helga gets caught, and she implicates me. I lose everything, my job, my lousy three hundred a month from Miss Mary, and the twenty-five hundred the Krauts owe me."

"What's to keep us from telling the police after the fact about your involvement in stealing the eye?"

"You don't think Helga's going to leave you alive to tell the tale." She laughed out loud. "I will take the necklace, though." She jerked the chain and the necklace came off in her hand. She dropped it in her pocket.

I lurched toward her, taking the chair with me and landing on my face on the cement floor. I heard and felt the crunch that could only mean a broken nose.

Cass struggled again against her ties. "Help her up. She's bleeding."

Archer set me upright and pulled a tissue from her sleeve. She tore it in half and stuffed a piece in each of my nostrils. "Serves her right."

"Never mind, Cass. She won't be around to enjoy the necklace." My voice sounded deep and nasal from restricted airflow, and my face felt numb.

The housekeeper cocked her head. "What are you saying?"

I swallowed hard and tasted blood. "I suspect you're right that Helga means to kill us. Don't you think she has the same fate in mind for you? She can't afford to leave you alive any more than she can us." The numbness was beginning to wear off. My whole face throbbed in time with my heartbeats.

She frowned and bit her lip. "You're just..." She pointed her finger in my face. "You're trying to get inside my head and I won't..." The basement door opened interrupting her, and

Gunther came down the steps. He nodded toward me. "What happened to her face?"

"She tried to jump me." She didn't say a word about the necklace she stole from Cass.

"There's been a change of plans. You get back upstairs."

"What now?"

"Just do as I say."

Archer stomped up the steps grumbling to herself. Something about Boris and Natasha in a Bullwinkle cartoon.

Gunther watched her close the door behind her. He turned his back to us and reached in his pocket. Was he about to pull out a gun or a knife? I held my breath and tried to avoid picturing what might happen next.

"Listen, Gunther." Cass was breathing rapidly and shaking her head. She started talking fast. "Take the eye. We know you're trying to do what you think is best for your country. We disagree about that, but let us go and we promise to work with you to come to a solution. You don't want to do this. We can help you. Whatever you want, just name it. I have money. Just take the eye and go."

Gunther pulled a switchblade knife out of his pocket. He stepped behind me, and I heard the click of the blade opening. Cass struggled so hard against the rope around her wrists she got one hand loose and desperately reached out to grab his arm. That's when he cut the knots on my hands and feet, then turned and sliced through Cass's ropes.

He looked up the stairs and listened for a second. "I warned you to let this play itself out. You're right. I have been saving you throughout your meddling. I'm undercover from BND, the German Federal Intelligence Service, the equivalent of your American CIA."

You can imagine my reaction. I expelled a big breath I'd been holding since he pulled out the switchblade. Holding my breath had been the only way to keep from screaming. I wiped cold sweat off my forehead with my sleeve. "Asshole! Why didn't you tell us this before?"

"We've been tracking Helga's gang for years, and she's close to delivering herself into our hands by stealing the eye. Your amateur sleuthing is about to interfere with thousands of hours of agent effort. If I had told you I'm with the BND, I couldn't trust you to keep your mouths shut. Now both of you sit down and stay quiet." He pointed to the back garden door where we came in. "I'm locking this door. I don't want you sneaking out and interfering any more than you already have." He locked the door and put the key in his pocket. "Do as I say and stay quiet down here. Your life depends on it." He went up the stairs and into the foyer.

Cass waited a few seconds, then began creeping up the stairs on all fours.

"What are you doing?"

"We can't just sit here and wait. Bella will walk right into a trap."

"But the German CIA guy or whatever he called himself will save her and us, won't he?"

"We can't count on that. He may shoot us to maintain his undercover persona with the National Identity Underground. Even if he does somehow thwart Helga's plan to steal the eye, he'll take it back to Germany and Egypt will never recover the bust." She climbed to the top step, turned the doorknob deliberately, and pushed the door open a crack.

We heard Helga's voice in the parlor. "Well?"

Gunther answered. "It's done.

"Good work."

Gunther's voice again. "Have you found any sign of a new combination?"

"No. We'll have to wait till she comes home."

"What about the housekeeper?"

"There's plenty of time for that. She might be helpful getting the combination out of the old lady. For now, just keep her away from the basement. She's in the kitchen making us some tea. Go in and keep an eye on her, and I'll do another search of the office. We may have overlooked Bella's hiding place for the new combination."

Cass eased the door shut and came back down the steps.

I didn't dare raise my voice above a whisper. "What do we do?"

"What we can't do is wait for Helga to decide our fate."

"What if she comes down to inspect Gunther's handiwork?"

"We'll have to jump her and take our chances."

"Which aren't great with both of them armed."

Cass nodded. "We need to look for a way outside. You sit on this chair while I try the window that faces the street. Moving around will make your nose bleed more." She dragged the other chair over and climbed on it. "It's painted shut."

"Can you break the glass?"

"They'd hear the noise before either of us could crawl out." She climbed down from the chair and began feeling around the walls. "There's a draft coming from somewhere behind these shelves." She moved canned goods and wine bottles aside. "It's an old chute from when the furnace burned coal. It will lead upward to the street beside the house. Can you help me take the shelves out?"

We cleared enough space to reveal a rusted iron door about three feet off the ground and measuring four feet square. The hinges groaned when Cass swung it open, and a black billow of coal dust swirled into the room. I froze, fully expecting Helga to charge down the stairs with guns blazing. No sound from the floor above.

Cass took my police flashlight and shined the beam up the chute. "It appears if we can crawl up the chute we'll come out on the sidewalk on the side of the house. There aren't any footholds.

You go inside the chute. I'll give you a boost. When you're outside you can pull me out." She made it sound easy.

I scrambled into the opening and stretched to my full height. My whisper echoed inside the metal shaft. "If you boost me about a foot and half, I can reach the latch." I had forgotten all about my damaged nose until the strain of crawling into the tight space and breathing the choking cloud of dust inside the chute amped up the throbbing.

Cass encircled my legs at the knees and hoisted me just enough that I was able to open the latch and crawl out to the sidewalk. Thank goodness I have passable upper body strength. I ducked back in the chute and grasped Cass's forearms and pulled her out.

We were both covered from head to toe with coal dust. Everywhere we stepped on the sidewalk we left a black trail. "Now can we go to the police?" I'd no sooner gotten the last word out when three police squad cars with blue lights flashing screeched to a stop in front of the house, blocking the street.

Chapter Fifteen

BELLA, CASS, AND I watched a female police detective and two uniformed cops march Helga, Gunther, and Frances Archer down the front steps. Gunther struggled against his handcuffs. "I tell you I'm with German Federal Intelligence. If you'll just check in my pocket you'll find my credentials."

The detective shoved him in the back seat of a squad car. "Just relax. We'll sort everything out down at the station. In the meantime, shut up." She slammed the door and slapped the roof, and the car pulled away from the curb. She put Helga and Archer in the back of another car.

"Cass, what about your necklace? Archer has it in her pocket."

Cass rubbed the abrasion on the back of her neck from when the housekeeper ripping off the chain. "The police will keep it as evidence against her."

"But they have to give it back to you, right?"

"I don't know."

The detective strode to where we were standing. Bella stuck out her hand. "Captain Carr, thank you so much for coming to our rescue. And most of all for giving credence to an old lady's rather wild story."

Captain Carr tucked a stray curl behind her ear. She wore her hair in a tight French Twist. It fit with her overall appearance of a put-together police professional. She wore a perfectly bland gray suit and a starched white blouse that almost managed to hide her killer body. I couldn't help comparing her appearance to the rumpled Inspector Saleem of the Luxor Police Department. I hoped the difference indicated we were safer in New York from all the intrigue around Nefertiti's eye.

Carr saluted. "Happy to serve. They gave up without much of a fight. They aren't what you'd call hardened criminal types.

Blondie's already crying diplomatic immunity, and you heard the guy claiming he's part of the German CIA. Your housekeeper put up the most resistance. She came after one of my men with a skillet." Carr checked her watch. "If the three of you will come to the 6th Precinct Station this morning, I'll have someone take your statements. In the meantime, avoid touching anything in the house, especially the safe, until I can get forensics here to go over the place." She turned, got in the passenger side of a police car, and rode away.

Cass took my face in her hands. "You realize your nose is broken. It's pointing a bit to the left." She touched it lightly, and I flinched. "We need to find you a doctor."

"You poor dear." Bella signaled her driver. "I'll go with you to Bellevue. We'll take my car."

The ER waiting room was packed with all kinds of human misery. Gunshot victims and traffic accidents got priority of course. We found three empty plastic chairs and scooted them close together. While we waited, Bella told the story of how she rescued us.

"In the middle of all the boring speeches, the thought occurred to me that I didn't have to wait for morning. I could drive past the house. If things were quiet, I could surmise that the thief hadn't shown himself yet, and I could go back to the Pierre and wait. If there was police activity, I would know you'd successfully sprung the trap. I drove past and saw lights in the house and shadows moving in the parlor, and I knew the plan must have failed somehow. I was worried for your safety...and Mrs. Archer's." She dropped her head in her hands. "I still can't believe the woman we have known and trusted for so long betrayed us. I'm glad Mary's not alive to see it." She rubbed her face. "Anyway, as I said, I saw the shadows in the parlor and they appeared to be male. I went to the Greenwich Village police station and told Captain Carr there were intruders in my home, and thank goodness she took me seriously."

Cass patted her hand. "Thank goodness for your initiative."

The nurse finally called my name and led me back to an oddly quiet barnlike room with two long rows of curtained cubicles. Doctors and nurses scurried in and out of the spaces. The scene looked like a movie speeded up to double time with the sound turned down. The nurse picked a cubicle for me and took my blood pressure. She didn't blink an eye at my looks. I was still covered with coal dust. After a few minutes a doctor in blue scrubs with a clipboard in his hand threw back the curtain and bustled in. He looked about twelve years old.

"Miss..." He consulted the clipboard. "...Morgan. Says here a broken nose." He turned my head from side to side. "Two pretty remarkable shiners too." He looked me up and down. "What happened? Did you get run over by a garbage truck?" He laughed at his own joke and didn't wait for an answer. "Believe me, I've seen that before." He put on rubber gloves and felt both sides of my nose and stuck his pinky up each nostril. It hurt so bad my eyes watered. I bit my lip to keep from yelling.

"Okay. It feels like a pretty clean break. Here's your choice. I can give you a shot to deaden your face before I set your nose. It'll take about an hour for full effect, then about four hours to wear off completely afterward. Or I can give it a quick snap and you're good to go."

I thought about Cass and Bella sitting in the crowded waiting room breathing in all the germs in New York City. "Just do it."

"Atta girl. Be right back." He was gone a while, and I had time to change my mind two or three times. The doctor brushed aside the curtain with the nurse on his heels carrying a tray with a nasal speculum, petroleum jelly, and gauze pads. He snapped on a fresh pair of rubber gloves. "Close your eyes." He sounded way too cheery.

Twenty seconds and it was all over. He popped my cartiladge back in place. It made a crunching sound exactly like the one I heard when I faceplanted on the floor in Bella's basement. "Just like that. And now, if you're lucky, you have your own complimentary built-in weather barometer. Every time the weather's about to change, your nose will ache."

"Seriously? I thought that was an old wives' tale."

"Some old wives' tales are true. Have a great life, Miss Morgan." And he was gone.

The nurse packed my nose, wrapped my face in gauze and tape, and began cleaning up the cubicle to get ready for the next patient.

"So I can go?"

"Yep."

Cass and Bella jumped to their feet when I came through the door into the waiting room. They both hugged me.

Cass brushed my hair out of my eyes. "Does it hurt? Can you tolerate going to the police station and getting our statements out of the way?"

"It's throbbing like a son of a bitch. Sorry, Bella."

"In Italian, figlio de puttana."

That made me laugh, and laughing made my nose hurt. "And yes, I can tolerate going to the police station."

The Greenwich Village 6th Precinct station on 10th Street is brand new with cookiecutter institutional architecture that lacks the charm of the old station. That old building looked more like a boutique hotel. The new lobby smelled like fresh paint mixed with human misery of the poor souls lining the walls on hard benches awaiting their fates. The desk sergeant said Captain Carr was expecting us. He pointed up with his pencil. "The detectives are on the second floor." He beckoned a man in line behind us. "Next!"

We went up the stairs to the second floor. The detective bullpen was a tangle of mismatched desks with men in ties and white shirts with their sleeves rolled up. Captain Carr brought each of us in turn into her office and took our statements, and a photographer snapped pictures of my face in bandages and the abrasion on the back of Cass's neck from Mrs. Archer stealing her necklace.

Carr walked us to the stairs. "That's all we need. A long limo from the German Embassy collected Helga twenty minutes before you arrived. She'll get off on diplomatic immunity, but she has to leave the country straight away. INTERPOL confirmed Gunther is with BND as he claimed. As for Frances, the ADA is on his way over. Based on your statements, I suspect we'll charge her with assault. Dr. Stillwell, we found a necklace matching your description in Frances's pocket, but I'm afraid we'll have to hold it as evidence."

Cass nodded.

"You're free to go back to your home, Miss Donatello. Forensics has wrapped up."

* * * * *

Bella unlocked the front door. "I'll make us some coffee, but first, after all you've been through, you'll want to see the eye." She led us down the hall to the study. She swung another of Mary's watercolors aside to reveal the wall safe. She rotated the combination wheel and opened the safe door. I held my breath. Cass entwined her fingers in mine.

Bella lifted out a rosewood box. It was smaller than I had pictured, the size and shape of a bar of Ivory Soap my gran favors for everything from washing dishes to taking a bath. The soap's slogan popped into my head, an echo from my childhood. *Ivory Soap. It floats.* I never understood why that would be something to advertise. You can find the soap easier? Why would my mind drift off to floating soap when the precious relic we've been searching for was finally right in front of us? I suppose thinking of my gran is my way of managing nerves.

Bella placed the box on the desk.

Cass's hand hovered over it. "May I?"

Bella nodded.

Cass ran a finger over the inscription incised on the lid and read aloud "Thutmose the Sculptor." She lifted the lid. Nefertiti's left eye gazed up at us. If a painted rock crystal could speak, this one would say, "What took you so long?"

Cass began humming under her breath. The three of us stood staring into the box.

Bella broke the spell by replacing the lid. "I see your passion." She returned the box to the safe, locked it, and spun the wheel. "I've decided to give you the eye. It's what Mary would have wanted."

Chapter Sixteen

A BREEZE OFF THE bay rippled through the live oak branches. Cass stretched out her long legs and turned her face up to Beaufort's soft April sun. "I could take a nap right here. I don't often suffer jet lag, but the last three weeks have left me feeling wrung out."

"But you did it. You negotiated an agreement for the return of Nefertiti to Egypt."

"You give me too much credit. It became a complicated back-and-forth among Egypt, Germany, and the Soviet Union. Once they decided on the size and shape of the negotiating table and who would be seated around it, your American State Department and the British Foreign Office brokered the deal. I wouldn't have had the patience. The German government has agreed to spend three hundred million dollars rebuilding Neues Museum in the Soviet sector, complete with a magnificent gallery all the Queen's own. When the restoration is complete, the bust of Nefertiti will live six months a year there and six months in the Egypt Museum in Cairo. In the meantime, a multi-national team of experts will attend her in Cairo and restore her eye. The chest and papyrus will stay in Cairo permanently."

"Was Helga involved?"

"Minister Stoph was there, but no sign of Helga. I suspect she's been quietly put to pasture."

"You'll be on television again, just like with Hatshepsut."

"I suppose, but for now let's not think about that. Let's enjoy the Old Burying Ground in Beaufort, North Carolina. Tell me about this place."

"I used to give ghost tours on Halloween night when I was in high school. How about a ghost tour?" I pulled her to her feet and guided her down the decomposed granite path. "This way, madam. It's much spookier at midnight, but we'll make do. Notice with most of the graves the feet point toward the east. People wanted to be facing the rising sun when they awoke on the morning of Judgement Day."

"Not so different from the ancient Egyptians' worship of Amun-Ra."

"We'll start with the most famous ghost. She was a two-year-old girl who died of yellow fever in the early 1800s. She was buried in a glass-topped coffin. You'll notice the toys covering her grave. People leave them believing she comes out at night to play. Gran says she's heard children's voices talking to her in the dark."

We cut across the sandy ground to an English Revolutionary War sailor's grave. "He drowned in the bay. He had told his buddies he wanted to be buried with his boots on, so they planted him upright. People have claimed to spy him standing at attention saluting Mad King George."

The path circled an ancient live oak. "And here lies Abigail Sloo, buried in a rum keg. Her parents brought her to Beaufort from London as a child, and when she grew into a young adult, she wanted to see her homeland. Her father, a sea captain, agreed to accompany her on the journey and swore to return her safely to Beaufort. The girl died on the trip home, and her father, not wanting to break his word to the mother, didn't bury her at sea but preserved her body in a keg of rum. When the time came, they buried her keg and all."

Cass picked a bench in the shade of the church building. "A fine tour. Let's sit a minute, darling. I want to talk. It's time we settled some things."

"That sounds ominous."

She pulled me down beside her. "You've wondered about the funding for my digs. I pay for them myself. I don't want to be beholden to any country or any meddling patron for how I conduct explorations. I told you money has never been an issue for me. I inherited a six-thousand-acre estate, Northfield Abbey, in England, complete with dark ancestral portraits on the walls and suits of armor. My cousin oversees the estate, and I receive a monthly stipend plus a cash disbursement whenever I need funding for a dig."

I tried to picture six thousand acres. "How many square miles is that?"

"About ten square miles of rolling meadows and forests dotted with tenant farms separated by rock fences."

"It sounds beautiful."

"Many would call it idyllic. I went there to be raised by my grandfather after my parents died in a plane crash."

"Oh, Cass."

"Yes, very sad, but I barely remember them. A series of nannies raised me. It seemed each time I got close to one my grandfather would let her go. He was a hard man. Ironically, it was from him I developed my love for archaeology. He was a bitter rival of Lord Carnarvon. Grandpapa even had a wing added to Northfield Abbey so he could boast of having more rooms at Northfield than Highclere's three hundred. "

"Lord Carnarvon is the guy who found Tutankhamun."

"Yes. My grandfather spent his life and a considerable amount of his wealth trying to outdo Carnarvon's Egyptian collection. Of course, when Carnarvon found Tutankhamun, he won the antiquities competition for good."

"Where is your grandfather's collection now?"

"I donated it to the Egyptian Museum in Cairo when he died."

I glanced at her sideways. "So are you a duchess?"

"Only wives of dukes are duchesses."

"But do I have to call you Lady Cassandra or something?" I was teasing, but Cass's reaction was dead serious.

"Of course not. That's precisely why I don't talk about Northfield Abbey. I don't want people assuming I'm some titled dilettante flitting from one ancient site to the next. I haven't lived at Northfield Abbey since I was twelve years old and went away to boarding school. I have no interest in ever going back, even to visit. There are too many painful memories there." She gazed around the cemetery. "Northfield and I have our own ghosts."

I waited for her to say more about the ghosts, but she didn't.

"Do you have a real place to live?"

"I have a townhouse in London. Otherwise in hotels." She squirmed on the bench. She was losing patience with being questioned. "What else do you want to know?"

"When you found Hatshepsut's golden coffin, instead of being elated, you were sad. I saw the same look on your face when you were about to enter the burial chamber at KV55."

"I suppose I experience empathy with who they were in life, real people with thoughts and feelings. Of course, the dead are in no position to object to our entering their final resting places, and those who could object, their descendants, give us explicit permission. But I always have a feeling of invading their privacy." She had the sorrowful look on her face again.

"But knowing you have solved the mystery of Nefertiti's missing eye must offset the sadness. You've proven the bust wasn't just a model but was meant to be a perfect finished work of art."

She touched her throat where Hatshepsut's cartouche would have been before Frances Archer stole it. "I suppose." She stood up. "It's getting chilly here in the shade. Let's walk." She linked her arm through mine. "Have I answered all your questions?"

I nodded. "I have a surprise for you." I reached in my pocket and pulled out her Hatshepsut necklace and held it in my palm. "Jessie's necklace. Bella and I kept bugging Captain Carr about it, and she released it to me after Frances Archer pleaded guilty to the assault charge. Bella insisted on paying to have the clasp fixed." I fastened it around Cass's neck. The diamond winked in the sunlight.

She grabbed me and hugged me tight. "Thank you, my darling." I felt the words rumble in her chest. "You know how much this means to me." She held me at arm's length. "Now I have a question for you. Will you go back to Egypt with me this summer?"

"Where? Back to Luxor?"

"No, this time to Alexandria."

I stuck a hand up. "Wait, don't tell me. Cleopatra."

"Yes. First we have to stop by Rome." She took my hand, and we started toward the front gate of the cemetery on Ann Street across from Mom and Gran's cottage. "A colleague has discovered a contemporaneous account of Cleopatra's death with clues about where she might be buried."

"Did she really commit suicide with an asp?"

"Doubtful, but that's what we will find out." I heard the familiar tone of excitement Cass's voice takes on when she's starting a new quest. "Before you give me an answer about going to Alexandria, this time I don't want you to leave at the end of summer. I want you to stay with me. Is that too selfish of me to ask?"

"What do you mean?"

"I want you with me, not back in New York. If finishing your last year of graduate school is important to you, I will get the dean to approve independent study."

"Of course I'll go, and of course I'll stay with you. It's what I've wanted all along."

Cass took a black velvet box out of her pocket. "Now I have a surprise for you." Inside was a gold necklace with an impossibly thin chain. The charm was the bust of Nefertiti with her slight smile and both her eyes.

THE END

About Jane Alden

Jane Alden was born and raised in a small Mississippi River Delta community in Arkansas. Everyone in town knew everyone else—their parents, and their grandparents before them. Though her father was a life-long cotton farmer, the family lived in town rather than on the farm, the only class difference in the all-white, all-protestant hamlet.

After graduating from the University of Arkansas, she moved to California and taught seventh grade English in a small central valley citrus-farming community. When she was recruited on the phone at U of A, she looked up Porterville, California, on the map, and it was only about an inch and a half north of Los Angeles, but it turned out the culture was closer to Arkansas or Oklahoma than to the bright lights and big city she craved. After two years teaching, she moved to Los Angeles and began a career in healthcare management. After many lucky circumstances and thanks to wonderful mentors, she ultimately became Chief Executive Officer at Los Angeles Children's Hospital, a mountain-top experience. After running a big organization for eight years, she became an executive coach, working with successful executives who want to be better leaders.

The Queen's Eye is Jane's sixth novel with Desert Palm Press and the second in a series recounting Cass and Ari's adventures in Egypt, following The Crystal's Curse. Jane and her partner live in Claremont, California, thirty miles east of Los Angeles. Their black lab, Lily, is the captain of the domestic ship.Connect with Jane:

Email: janealdenauthor@gmail.com
Twitter: @janealden5
Facebook: JaneAldenBooks

Note to Readers:

Thank you for reading a book from Desert Palm Press. We appreciate you as a reader and want to ensure you enjoy the reading process. We would like you to consider posting a review on your preferred media sites and/or your blog or website.

For more information on upcoming releases, author interviews, contests, giveaways and more, please sign up for our newsletter and visit us at Desert Palm Press: www.desertpalmpress.com and "Like" us on Facebook: Desert Palm Press.

Bright Blessings

Printed in the USA
CPSIA information can be obtained
at www.ICGtesting.com
LVHW020214100624
782802LV00016B/299